CW00525426

THE
MINDWARPERS

ERIC FRANK RUSSELL

Dover Publications, Inc.
Mineola, New York

Bibliographical Note

This Dover edition, first published in 2017, is an unabridged republication of the work originally published by Lancer Books, Inc., New York, in 1965.

Library of Congress Cataloging-in-Publication Data

Names: Russell, Eric Frank, 1905–1978, author.
Title: The mindwarpers / Eric Frank Russell.
Description: Mineola, New York : Dover Publications, 2017.
Identifiers: LCCN 2016057512| ISBN 9780486814476 (paperback) | ISBN 0486814475
Subjects: | BISAC: FICTION / Science Fiction / Adventure. | FICTION / Science
   Fiction / Military. | GSAFD: Science fiction.
Classification: LCC PR6035.U66 M56 2017 | DDC 823/.914—dc23 LC record available at https://lccn.loc.gov/2016057512

Manufactured in the United States by LSC Communications
81447501   2017
www.doverpublications.com

ONE:

THE GOVERNMENTAL research establishment, the very heart of the country's scientific effort, was huge and formidable by any standard, even that of the technological twentieth century. By comparison, Fort Knox and Alcatraz, the Bastille and the Kremlin were as frontier forts built with wood logs. Yet it was vulnerable. Hostile eyes had examined what little could be seen of it, hostile minds had carefully considered what little was known about it, after which the entire complex became less safe than a moth-eaten tent.

The outer wall stood forty feet high. It was eight feet thick, of granite blocks sealed and faced with aluminous cement. Satin-smooth, there wasn't a toe-hold on it, not even for a spider. Beneath the base of the wall, thirty-six feet down, ran a sensitive microphone system, wired in duplicate, intended to thwart any human moles who might try to burrow their way inside. Those who had designed the wall had been firmly convinced that fanatics are capable of anything and that nothing was too far-fetched to justify counter-measures.

In the great length of this quadrilateral wall were only two breaks, a narrow one at the front for the entry and exit of personnel, a wider one at the back for trucks bringing supplies or removing products. Both gaps were protected by three forty-ton hardened steel doors, as massive as dock gates, mechanically operated and incapable of standing open more than one at a time. Each door was attended by its own squad of guards, big, tough, sour-faced men who in the opinion of all those who had dealings with them had been specially chosen for their mean, suspicious natures.

Exit was less difficult than entry. Invariably armed

with a pass-out permit, the departer merely suffered the delay of waiting for each door to close behind him before the one in front could open. Movement in the opposite direction, inward, was the real chore. If one were an employee well-known to the guards one could get through subject to tedious waits at three successive doors plus a possible check on whether one's pass—the pattern of which was changed at unpredictable intervals—bore the current design.

But the stranger had it tough no matter how high his rank, important his bearing or authoritative the documents he presented. He would certainly suffer a long and penetrating inquisition at the hands of the first squad of guards. If his questioners were not thoroughly satisfied—and most times they were satisfied with nothing in heaven or on earth—the visitor was likely to be searched right down to the skin. Any protest on his part usually resulted in the search being extended to include close inspection of his physical apertures. Anything found that was deemed suspicious, superfluous, unreasonable, inexplicable or not strictly necessary for the declared purpose of the visit was confiscated on the spot and returned to the owner when he took his departure.

And that was only the first stage of this bureaucratic purgatory. At the next door the second squad of guards specialized in concocting objections to entry not thought up by the first guards. Its members were not above belittling the security consciousness and search proficiency of the first guards and insisting upon a second "more expert" search. This could and sometimes did include removal of the dental plates and careful examination of the naked mouth, a tactic inspired by the known development of a camera the size of a cigarette's filter-tip.

Guard squad number three had the worst skeptics of the lot. Its members had an infuriating habit of detaining twice-passed incomers while they checked with squads one and two was to whether this, that or the other question had been asked and, if so, what replies had been given. They had a tendency to doubt the truth of some replies, throw scorn upon the plausibility of others and seek contradictions over which they could foam at the mouth. Full details of searches were often demanded by them´ and any omission in search-technique was made good then and there even if the victim had to strip himself stark naked for the third time in thirty minutes. Guard squad number three also possessed but seldom used an X-ray machine, a polygraph, a stereoscopic camera, a fingerprinting outfit and several other sinister devices.

The great protective wall surrounding the plant was in keeping with what lay within. Offices, departments, machine shops and laboratories were rigidly compartmentalized with steel doors and stubborn guards blocking the way from one well-defined area to another. Each self-contained section was identified by the color of its corridors and doors, the higher up the spectrum the greater the secrecy and priority in security assigned to a given area.

Workers in yellow-door areas were not allowed to pass through blue doors. Toilers behind blue doors could "go slumming" as they called it by entering a yellow or lower priority area but were strictly forbidden to stick their noses the other side of purple doors. Not even the security guards could go beyond a black door without a formal invitation from the other side. Only the black-area men and the President and God Almighty could amble around other sections as they pleased and explore the entire plant.

Throughout the whole of this conglomeration ran its intricate nervous system in the form of wires buried in the walls, ceilings and, in some cases, under the floors; wires linking up with general alarm-bells and sirens, door-locking mechanisms, delicate microphones and television-scanners. All the watching and listening was done by black-area snoopers. The plant's inmates had long accepted the necessity of being continually heard and seen even when in the toilet—for where better than the little room in which to memorize, copy or photograph classified data?

Such trouble, ingenuity and expense was useless from the viewpoint of outside and unfriendly eyes. The place was, in fact, a veritable Singapore, wide open to attack from an unseen and unexpected quarter. There was no good reason why its weak spot should have passed by

7

unobserved except, perhaps, that the apprehensive can be so finicky as to overlook the obvious.

In spite of hints and forewarnings the obvious was overlooked. The people at the top of the research center's plant were highly qualified experts, each in his own field and therefore ignorant of other fields. The chief bacteriologist could talk for hours about a new and virulent germ without knowing whether Saturn has two moons or ten. The head of the ballistics department could draw graphs of complicated trajectories without being able to say whether an okapi belongs to the deer, horse or giraffe family. The entire place was crammed with experts of every kind save one—the one who could see and understand a broad hint when it became visible.

For example, nobody found any significance in the fact that while the plant's employees bore security measures, searchings and snoopings with resigned fortitude, most of them detested the color-area system. Color had become a prestige symbol. The yellow-area man considered himself downgraded with respect to his blue-area counterpart even though getting the same salary. The man who worked behind red doors viewed himself as several cuts above a white-door man. And so on.

Women, always the socially conscious sex, boosted this attitude to the utmost. Female workers and the wives of male workers adopted in their outside relations a farmyard pecking-order based upon the color of the area in which they or their husbands worked. The wives of black-area workers were tops and proud of it; those of white-area men were bottom and riled by it. The sweet smile and cooing voice and feline display of claws was the normal form of greeting among them.

Such a state of affairs was accepted by all and sundry as "just one of those things." But it was not just one of those things; it was direct evidence that the plant was occupied and operated by human beings who were not robots made of case-hardened steel. The absent expert—a topflight psychologist—could have recognized this fact with half an eye even though he might not know a venturi-tube from a rocket nose-cap.

That was where the real weakness lay: not in concrete, granite or steel, not in mechanisms or electronic devices, not in routines or precautions or paperwork, but in flesh and blood.

Haperny's resignation caused more irritation than alarm. Forty-two years old, dark-haired and running slightly to fat, he was a red-area expert specializing in high-vacuum phenomena. All who knew him regarded him as clever, hard-working, conscientious and as emotional as a plaster statue. So far as was known little interested Haperny beyond his work. The fact that he was a stodgy and determined bachelor was considered proof that he had nothing for which to live outside of his work.

Bates, the head of his department, and Laidler, the chief security officer, summoned him for an interview. They were sitting side by side behind a big desk when he lumbered in and blinked at them through thick-lensed glasses. Bates put a sheet of paper on the desk and poked it forward.

"Mr. Haperny, I've had this passed to me. Your resignation. What's the idea?"

"I want to leave," said Haperny, fidgeting.

"Obviously! But why? Have you found a better position someplace else? If so, with whom? We are entitled to know."

Haperny shuffled his feet and looked unhappy. "No, I haven't got another job. Haven't looked for one, either. Not just yet. Later on perhaps."

"Then why have you decided to go?" Bates demanded.

"I've had enough."

"Enough?" Bates was incredulous. "Enough of what?"

"Of working here."

"Let's get this straight," said Bates. "You're a valuable man and you've been with us fourteen years. Up to now you appear to have been content. Your work has been first-class and nobody has criticized it or you. If you could maintain that record you'd be secure for the rest of your natural life. Do you really want to throw away a safe and rewarding job?"

"Yes," said Haperny, dully determined.

"And with nothing better in prospect?"

"That's right."

Leaning back in his chair, Bates stared at him speculatively. "Know what I think? I think you're feeling the wear and tear. I think you ought to see the medic."

"I don't want to," declared Haperny. "What's more, I don't have to. And I'm not going to."

"He might certify that you're suffering from the nervous strain of overwork. He might recommend that you be given a good, long rest," urged Bates. "You could then take an extended vacation on full pay. Go fishing somewhere quiet and peaceful and come back in due course feeling like a million dollars."

"I'm not interested in fishing."

"Then what the devil are you interested in? What do you intend to do after you've left here?"

"I want to amble around for a time. Wherever the fancy takes me. I want to be free to go where I please."

Frowning to himself, Laidler chipped in with, "Do you plan to leave this country?"

"Not immediately," said Haperny. "Not unless I have to."

"Have to? Any reason why you might have to?" Getting no answer, Laidler went on, "Your personal record shows that you have never been issued a passport. It's my duty to warn you that you may have to face some mighty awkward questions if ever you do apply for one. You possess information that could be useful to an enemy, and the government cannot afford to ignore that fact."

"Are you implying that I might be persuaded to sell what I know?" growled Haperny, showing ire.

"Not at all, not in present circumstances," said Laidler, evenly. "Right now your character is above reproach. Nobody doubts your loyalty. But—"

"But what?"

"Circumstances can change. A fellow wandering aimlessly around without a job, with no source of income, must eventually come to the end of his savings. He then experiences his first taste of poverty. His ideas start altering. He has second thoughts about a lot of things he once took for granted. See what I mean?"

"I don't contemplate becoming a hobo. I'll get a job sometime, when I'm good and ready."

10

"Is that so?" interjected Bates, raising a sardonic eyebrow. "What do you think the average employer is going to say when you walk in and ask could he use a high-vacuum physicist?"

"My qualifications don't prevent me from washing dishes," Haperny pointed out. "If you don't mind, I'd like to be left to solve my own problems in my own way. This is a free country, isn't it?"

"We want to keep it that way," put in Laidler.

Bates let go a deep sigh and opined, "If a fellow insists on suddenly going crazy, I can't stop him. So I'll accept this resignation and pass it along to headquarters. No doubt they'll take a grim view of it. If they decide that you are to be shot at dawn it'll be up to them to tend to it." He waved a hand in dismissal. "All right, leave it with me."

Haperny departed and Laidler said, "Did you notice his expression when you made that crack about being shot at dawn? He knew you were kidding, of course, but all the same he seemed to go sort of strained looking. Maybe he's scared of something."

"Imagination," Bates scoffed. "I was watching him myself. He looked normal enough in his stubborn, owl-eyed way. I think he's belatedly jumpy because Nature's caught up with him."

"Meaning?"

"He's been sexually retarded but at last has outgrown it. Even at forty-two it's not too late to do something about it. Bet you he leaves here at full gallop, like an eager bull. He'll keep running until he finds a suitable mate. Then he'll get coupled and cool down and want his job back."

"You may be right," conceded Laidler, "but I wouldn't care to put money on it. I feel instinctively that Haperny is badly worried. It would be nice to know what's causing it."

"Not the worrying type," Bates assured. "Never has been and never will be. What he wants is a roll in the hay. No law against it, is there?"

"Sometimes I think there ought to be," said Laidler, mysteriously. "Anyway, when a high-grade expert suddenly decides to take off into the blue we can't safely assume that today's date marks the opening of his breeding season. There may be a deeper and more dangerous reason. We need to know about that."

"So?"

"He'll have to be watched until we're satisfied that he's doing no harm and intends none. A couple of counter-espionage agents will have to keep tab on him. That costs money."

"Will it come out of your wallet?"

"No."

"Then what do you care?"

"Since you put it that way," said Laidler, "I'll admit that I don't give a damn."

The news about Haperny drifted around the plant, causing a few raised eyebrows and some perfunctory discussion. In the canteen Richard Bransome, a green-area metallurgist, talked about it with his co-worker Arnold Berg. In the future both men were to be the unwilling subjects of greater mysteries, though, of course, neither suspected it at this time.

"Arny, have you heard that Haperny is getting out?"

"Yes. Told me so himself a few minutes ago."

"H'm! Has he become bored with the scenery? Or has someone offered him more money?"

"His story," said Berg, "is that he's become sick of regimentation and wants to run loose a while. It's the gypsy in him."

"Strange," mused Bransome. "I never thought of him as a fidget. Seemed to me as stolid and as solid as a lump of rock."

"Wanderlust does look out of character for him," Berg admitted. "But you know the old saying: still waters run deep."

"You may be right. I have moments of getting tired of routine—but not tired enough to throw up a good job."

"You have a wife and two kids to keep," Berg pointed out. "Haperny has nobody to consider but himself. He's free to do as he likes. If he wants to switch from scientific research to garbage collecting, I say good luck to him. Somebody's got to move our garbage, else we'd be stuck with it. Have you ever thought of that?"

"My mind dwells on higher things," said Bransome, virtuously.

"It'd drop to lower levels if the junk were piling up in your backyard," Berg retorted.

Ignoring that, Bransome said, "Haperny is stodgy but no dope. He's got a plodding but brilliant mind. If he's taking off it's for a reason better than the one he's seen fit to make public."

"Such as?"

"I don't know. I can only guess. Maybe he's been given another official job elsewhere and is under strict orders to keep his mouth shut."

"Could be. In this uncertain world anything is possible. Someday I may vanish myself—and make good as a strip-teaser."

"What, with that paunch?"

"It will add to the interest," said Berg, patting it fondly.

"Have it your own way." Bransome pondered a short time, then went on, "Now that I come to think of it, this place has been getting its knocks of late."

"Anything regarded as a burden upon the taxpayer is sure to be kicked from time to time," offered Berg. "There is always somebody ready to howl about the expenditure."

"I wasn't considering the latest cost-cutting rigmarole. I was still thinking about Haperny."

"His departure won't wreck the works," asserted Berg. "It'll be no more than a darned inconvenience. Takes time and trouble to replace an expert. The supply of specialists isn't unlimited."

"Precisely! And it seems to me that these days the time and trouble are taken more often."

"How d'you mean?"

"I've been here eight years. For the first six of those our staff losses were no more or less than one would expect. Fellows reached the age of sixty-five and exercised their right to retire on pension. Others agreed to continue working but fell ill or dropped dead sometime later. A few young ones pegged out from natural

13

causes or got themselves killed in accidents. Some people were transferred to more urgent work elsewhere. And so on. As I said, the losses were reasonable."

"Well?" prompted Berg.

"Take a look at the last couple of years and you'll see a somewhat different picture. In addition to the normal sequence of deaths, retirements and transfers we've had sudden disappearances for unusual reasons. There was McLain and Simpson, for example. Took a vacation up the Amazon, evaporated into thin air and no trace of them has been found."

"That was eighteen months ago," Berg contributed. "It is a good bet that they're dead. Could be anything: drowning, fever, snake-bite or eaten alive by piranhas."

"Then there was Jacobert. Married a wealthy dame who had inherited a big cattle spread in Argentina. He goes there to help manage the place. How's that for a round peg in a square hole? As an exceptionally able chemical engineer he wouldn't know which end of a cow does the mooing."

"He can learn. He'd be doing it for love and money and I cannot imagine better reasons. I'd do the same myself, given the chance."

"And Henderson," continued Bransome. "Another case like Haperny's. Took off on a whim. I heard a rumor that some time later he was found operating a hardware store out west."

"And I heard another rumor that immediately he was found he took off again," said Berg.

"Which reminds me, talking about rumors: there was that one about Muller. Found shot. The verdict was accidental death. Rumor said it was suicide. Yet Muller had no known reason to kill himself and definitely he wasn't the type to be careless with a gun."

"Are you suggesting he was murdered?" asked Berg, giving the other a quizzical look.

"I'm suggesting only that his death was peculiar, to say the least. For the matter of that, so was Arvanian's a couple of months ago. Drove his car off a dockside and into forty feet of water. They said he must have suffered a blackout. He was thirty-two, an athletic type and in excellent health. The blackout theory doesn't look plausible to me."

"What are your medical qualifications?"

"None," Bransome admitted.

"The fellow who came up with the blackout notion was a fully qualified doctor. Presumably he knew what he was talking about."

"Not saying he didn't. What I am saying is that he made an intelligent guess and not a diagnosis. A guess is a guess is a guess, no matter who makes it."

"Could you offer a better one?"

"Yes—if Arvanian had been a heavy drinker. In that case I'd think it likely he met his end as result of driving while drunk. But he wasn't a boozer as far as I know. Neither was he a diabetic. Maybe he fell asleep at the wheel."

"That could happen," Berg agreed. "I did it myself once. It wasn't brought on by tiredness, either. It was caused by the sheer monotony of driving on a long, lonely road in the dark, hearing the steady hum of the tires and watching the headlight beams swaying. I yawned a few times, then—*ker-rash!* Found myself sprawled in a ditch with a large lump on my head. The experience shook me up for weeks, I can tell you!"

"Arvanian hadn't done a long, monotonous drive. He'd covered exactly twenty-four miles."

"So what? He could have been drowsy after a hard day's work. Possibly he hadn't been sleeping well of late. A few spoiled nights can make a man muddle-minded and ready to bed down anywhere, even behind a wheel."

"You're right about that, Arny. As the father of two kids I've had a taste of it. Lack of sleep can pull a man down. It shows in the way he does his work." Bransome tapped the table by way of emphasis. "It didn't show in Arvanian's work."

"But—"

"Furthermore, he was supposed to be on his way home. The dockside was out of line from his direct route by three miles or more. He must have made a detour to get there. Why?"

"I don't know."

"Neither do I. It looks rather like suicide. Quite pos-

15

sibly it wasn't. Nobody knows what it was. I feel entitled to say there was something decidedly strange about it and that's as far as I go."

"You've got a prying mind," said Berg. "Why don't you set up in business as a private investigator?"

"More hazards and less security," responded Bransome, smiling. He glanced at his watch. "Time we returned to the treadmill."

Two months later Berg disappeared. During the ten days preceding his vanishing he had been quiet, thoughtful and uncommunicative. Bransome, who worked closest to him, noticed it and for the first few days put it down to a spell of moodiness. But as the other's attitude persisted and grew into something more like wary silence, he became curious.

"Sickening for something?"

"Eh?"

"I said are you sickening for something? You've become as broody as an old hen."

"I'm not aware of it," said Berg, defensively.

"You're aware of it now because I've just told you. Sure you feel all right?"

"There's nothing the matter with me," Berg asserted. "A fellow doesn't have to yap his head off all the time."

"Not saying he does."

"Okay, then. I'l talk when I feel like it and keep shut when I feel like it."

After that the silence increased. On his last day at the plant Berg uttered not a word other than those strictly necessary. The next day he failed to appear. In the mid afternoon Bransome was summoned to Laidler's office. Laidler greeted him with a frown, pointed to a chair.

"Sit down. You work along with Arnold Berg, don't you?"

"That's right."

"Are you particularly friendly with him?"

"Friendly enough but I wouldn't say especially so."

"What d'you mean by that?"

"Bransome and Berg Incorporated is what the others jokingly call us," Bransome explained. "We get on

16

very well together at our work. I understand him and he understands me. Each knows he can depend upon the other. As partners in work we suit each other topnotch —but that's all it amounts to."

"Purely an industrial relationship?"

"Yes."

"You have never extended it into private life?"

"No. Outside of our work we had little in common."

"Humph!" Laidler was disappointed. "He hasn't reported today. He hasn't applied for official leave. Have you any idea why he's not here?"

"Sorry, I haven't. Yesterday he said nothing to indicate that he might not turn up. Maybe he's ill."

"Doesn't seem so," said Laidler. "We've had no medical certificate from him."

"There hasn't been much time for that. If one has been mailed today you wouldn't get it until tomorrow."

"He could have phoned," Laidler insisted. "He knows how to use a telephone. He's grown up now and has the right to wash his own neck. Or if he's bedbound somewhere he could have got someone to phone for him."

"Perhaps he's been rushed to the hospital in no condition to give orders or make requests," Bransome suggested. "That does happen to some people occasionally. Anyway, the telephone operates both ways. If *you* were to call *him*—"

"A most ingenious idea. It does you credit." Laidler sniffed disdainfully. "We called his number a couple of hours ago. No answer. We called a neighbor who went upstairs and hammered on the door of his apartment. No reply. The neighbor got the super to open up with his master key. They had a look inside. Nobody there. The apartment is undisturbed and nothing looks wrong. The super doesn't know what time Berg went out or, for the matter of that, whether he came home last night." He rubbed his chin, mused a bit. "Berg's a divorcee. Do you know if he has a girl friend currently?"

Bransome thought back. "A few times he's mentioned meeting some girl he liked. About four or five in all. But his interest didn't seem to be more than casual. As far as I know he didn't pursue them or go steady with

17

any of them. He was rather a cold fish in his attitude toward women; most of them sensed it and reciprocated."

"In that case it doesn't seem likely that he's overslept in a love-nest." Laidler thought again and added, "Unless he has resumed relations with his former wife."

"I doubt it."

"Has he mentioned her of late?"

"No. I don't think he has given her a thought for several years. According to him they were hopelessly incompatible but didn't realize it until after marriage. She wanted passion and he wanted peace. She called it mental cruelty and heaved him overboard. A couple of years afterward she married again."

"His personal record shows that he has no children. He has named his mother as next of kin. She's eighty years old."

"Perhaps she has cracked up and he's rushed to her bedside," Bransome suggested.

"As I said before, he's had all day to phone and tell us. He hasn't phoned. Moreover, there's nothing wrong with his mother. We checked on that a short time ago."

"Then I can't help you any further."

"One last question," persisted Laidler. "Do you know of anyone else in this plant who might be well-informed about Berg's private life? Anyone who shares his tastes and hobbies? Anyone who might have gone around with him evenings and weekends?"

"Sorry, I don't. Berg wasn't unsociable but he wasn't gregarious either. Seemed satisfied with his own company outside of working hours. I've always regarded him as a very self-contained kind of individual."

"Well, if he walks in tomorrow, wearing a big, fat grin, he'll need all his self-containment, I can tell you. He'll be on the carpet for playing hookey without telling anyone. It's against the rules and it gives us trouble. Rules aren't made to be broken—and we don't like trouble." He eyed Bransome with irritated authority and ended, "If he fails to reappear and if you should hear about him from any source whatever, it will be your duty to inform me at once."

"I'll do that," Bransome promised.

18

Leaving the office, he returned to the green area, his mind mulling the subject of Berg. Should he have told Laidler about Berg's recent surliness? Of what use if he had? He could not offer an explanation for it; he couldn't imagine a reason except, perhaps, that all unwittingly he had done something or said something that had upset Berg. But most definitely Berg was not the type to nurse a grievance in silence. Even less was he the kind to spend a day sulking in some hiding-place, like a peevish child.

Pondering these matters, he remembered Berg's odd remark of two months ago, "Someday I may vanish myself—and make good as a strip-teaser." Had that been an idle comment or did it have a hidden significance? In the latter case, what had Berg meant by "strip-teaser"? There was no way of telling.

"To blazes with it!" said Bransome to himself. "I've other things to worry about. Anyway, he's sure to turn up tomorrow with a plausible excuse."

But Berg did not appear next day or any day thereafter. He had gone for keeps.

19

TWO:

IN THE next couple of months three more top-graders took their departure in circumstances that could and should have set all the alarm-bells ringing—but didn't. One, like Berg, lit out for the never-never land, apparently on a whim. The other two left more formally after offering weak, unconvincing excuses that served only to arouse the ire of Bates and Laidler. The latter felt impotent to do anything about it but gripe. In a free country a man makes his own moves to suit himself without being arrested and imprisoned for incomplete candidness and without being compelled to undergo a prefrontal lobotomy.

Then came the turn of Richard Bransome. Appropriately enough, the world fell about his ears on Friday the Thirteenth. Up to then it had been a pleasant, comfortable world despite its shortcomings. There had been, on occasion, routine and boredom, rivalries and fears, the thousand and one petty pinpricks such as most men have to endure. But life had been lived, a life full of those little taken-for-granted items that are never fully appreciated until suddenly they vanish forever.

In the morning the regular departure of the 8:10 train. The same faces in the same seats, the same rustle of unfolding newspapers and low mutter of conversation. Or in the evening, the anticipatory homecoming along a tree-lined avenue where always some neighbor was polishing a car or cutting a lawn. The pup gamboling around him on the front path. Dorothy's face, flushed with kitchen-heat, smiling a welcome while the two kids hung from his wrists and demanded that he rotate and make carnival noises.

All these petty but precious treasures that made

each day: at one stroke they lost solidity, actuality, realness. They blurred and went right out of focus, fading like reluctant ghosts undecided whether to stay or go. They retreated from him, leaving him in an awful mental solitude. He made a frantic grasp at them with all the desire of his shocked mind and momentarily they came back—only to fade away again.

Words started it, plain, ordinary words in an overheard conversation. He was homeward bound on a cool evening that held first hint of coming winter. Thin streamers of mist crawled through the growing dark. As always, he had to change trains and wait twelve minutes for the connection. Following his long-established habit, he went to the snack bar for coffee. He sat at the counter, on the right-hand stool, and gave the order he'd given times without number.

"Coffee, black."

Nearby two men sat nursing cups of coffee and talking in desultory manner. They looked like long-distance night truckers soon to go on duty. One of them had a peculiar drawling accent that Bransome could not identify.

"It's fifty-fifty," said the drawler, "even if it had been done yesterday. The cops never solve more than half the murders. They admit it themselves."

"Oh, I don't know," argued the other. "Figures can be misleading. For instance, how many times have they pinched a character who has done more than one job, maybe a dozen jobs?"

"How d'you mean?"

"Look, let's see things as they really are and not as they ought to be. Nobody is executed for committing murder and that's an incontrovertible fact. If a fellow is sent to his death it's for quite a different reason. It's because they know he's a murderer and can prove it and have proved it. He's guilty of the one and only real crime there is, namely that of being found out. So they fry him."

"So?"

"For all they know he's done several other murders that they haven't heard about or can't prove. Those remain in the limbo of unsuspected or unsolved crimes. What difference would it make if they could pin them

on him? None whatever! They can't exeute him several
more times. When he pays the price for one killing he
pays for all his killings." The speaker sipped coffee
meditatively. "The true facts aren't available and
never will be; but if they were they might show that a
murderer's chances of getting away with it are as good
as eighty in a hundred."

"I'll give you that," conceded the drawler. "They
reckon that this one was done about twenty years ago.
That gives the culprit a whale of a start."

"How'd you come to get mixed up in it?"

"I told you. The floods had undermined this big tree.
It was teetering over the road, at a dangerous angle.
Made me duck my head in the cab as I edged past. A
few miles farther on I found a prowl-car. I stopped
and warned its crew that fifty tons of timber were
threatening to block the road. They raced off for a
look."

"And then?"

"A couple of days later a state trooper came
clunking into the depot and asked for me. He told me
the tree had been pulled down, cut up and hauled away.
Said they'd found human bones under its roots, believed
to be female and buried about twenty years. They're
waiting for some expert to look them over, the bones I
mean." He gulped coffee and scowled at the wall. "He
said the skull had been bashed in. Then he stared at me
as if I was the very guy they were looking for and he
wanted to know how many years I've been driving
along that particular road and whether I can remember seeing anything suspicious 'way back when he was
trundling around in his kiddie-car."

"But you refused to squeal?" asked the other, grinning.

"Couldn't tell him a thing. He took my home address
in case I'm wanted again. Maybe they'll be watching
for me next time I go through Burleston. That's what I
get for looking after the public interest."

Burleston.

Burleston!

The listener at the other end of the counter gazed
blankly at his coffee cup. It drooped in fingers from
which strength was flowing away like invisible water.

Burleston! The cup threatened to spill. He prevented it from slopping over only by a great effort of will-power, lowered it to its saucer, then slid off his stool and went out. The truckers ignored him as he left. He walked slowly, weak at the knees, with cold thrills lancing up his spine, his brain awhirl.

Burleston!

I am Richard Bransome, a highly-qualified metallur-gist in government employ. I have the confidence of my superiors, the friendship of my colleagues and neigh-bors, the love of my wife and two kids and a pup. Be-fore I was assigned to top secret work my background was thoroughly investigated by those trained to make a one hundred percent job of it. My record is clean, my past is spotless. There are no skeletons in my cup-board.

No skeletons?

Oh, God, why do the dead have to arise from their graves and point a finger into the present time? Why can't they lie in peace forever and let the living con-tinue to live in similar peace?

He stood dazedly, with unseeing eyes, while his train rumbled in without his being fully aware of its arrival. Conditioned legs carried him into his usual car much as they might have taken a blind man. He fumbled around uncertainly, found his seat, sat in it and hardly knew what he was doing.

Why did I kill Arline?

The coach was fairly full, as always. He had the same faces opposite and all around. They had greeted his entry with the customary nods and made ready for the customary idle chat.

The man facing him, Farmiloe, folded an evening pa-per, gave his preliminary cough and commented, "Been a good day though I say it myself. Trade's picking up quite a piece. High time we had an uprise to compen-sate for—" His voice broke off, came back on a slightly higher note. "You feeling ill, Bransome?"

"Me?" Bransome gave a visible jerk. "No, I'm all right."

"You don't look it," Farmiloe informed. "You're white enough to have had a shower." He leaned sidewise, gave a fat chuckle as he nudged Connelly, the man next to him. "Hear what I just said? I said Bransome's white enough to have had a shower."

"He doesn't look so good at that," said Connelly, refusing to be overwhelmed by the other's wit. Eyeing Bransome warily, he moved his knees away. "Don't you be sick in my lap."

"I'm okay. There's nothing wrong with me." The words came out as if he were using somebody else's voice.

Why did I kill Arline?

Farmiloe let the subject drop and switched to yammering about rises and falls of business. All the time he gazed at Bransome with big white eyes, slightly protruding. He appeared to be half-expecting an unpleasant something that he did not want to happen. For that matter, so did Connelly, though in a less obvious way. They had the air of men hoping to escape a minor crisis, such as being called upon to give first aid to somebody rolling in agony upon the floor.

The train thundered onward while conversation petered out and the three sat uncomfortably in an atmosphere of suspense. None of them had another word to say. Eventually a string of lights slid past the windows, slowed, came to a halt. Voices sounded in the misty darkness outside. Somebody started trundling a squeaky hand-truck up near the front of the train. Connelly and Farmiloe looked expectantly at Bransome who sat absent-eyed, unconscious of their attention.

After a few seconds Farmiloe leaned forward and tapped Bransome's knee. "Unless you've moved your home since yesterday, this is your station."

"Is it?" Bransome looked incredulous. He rubbed condensation from the window and peered through. "So it is!" Grabbing his leather briefcase, he forced a false smile onto his face, hastened toward the exit. "Must have been daydreaming."

As he went through the door he heard Connelly say, "Nightmaring would be more accurate."

Then he found himself standing on the concrete watching the train pull out. Its brilliantly lit cars rolled past him one by one, gathering speed as they

24

went. He could see row after row of passengers chatting, reading papers or lolling back half asleep. None of these had anything to worry about, not really. Their minds were occupied with matters comparatively trivial. Wonder what's for dinner tonight? Feel like a nice quiet evening watching television: will Mabel want to go out or will she be content to stay in? Will Old Soandso sign those papers tomorrow without quibbling? They were lazy and complacent just as he had been on his homeward journeys—until today.

But now the hunt was up and he, Bransome, was the quarry. Of all that passing trainload he alone knew the fear of the pursued. It was not the adventurous thrill that some claimed it to be. It was heart-knocking and mind-disturbing, a psychological upheaval the like of which he had never known. At the end of the trail, quite possibly, stood the prize awarded to long-distance runners: the electric chair, the scientific monstrosity that the criminal fraternity called the hot squat. He could picture it in his mind's eye and the vision did nothing to encourage tranquillity.

There was no escape from this predicament, or none that he could think up right now. The shock was too recent for him to be capable of cool, logical thought. Walking away from the station he turned the corner of an avenue without any real consciousness of where he was going. An auto-pilot created in his mind by long conditioning was steering him homeward. He saw the illuminated windows of neighbor's houses, a spectacle he had always regarded as evidence of life, but now he viewed them as no more than mere lights—because his thoughts were of death.

Bones under the roots of a tree that could and should have shadowed them for another century. Bones that could and should have remained there unsuspected and untouched until events had drifted too far into the past for any man to trace into the present. There seemed to be some sort of devilish perversity in the so-called laws of chance, a gross distortion of the probability-factor to the detriment of the guilty. So out of this world's multi-million trees one especial tree must topple, thereby starting the manhunt.

Young Jimmy Lindstrom passed him, towing a red-

25

painted toy truck at the end of a cord, and sang out, "Hi, Mr. Bransome!"

"Hi!" he responded mechanically, forgetting to add, "Jimmy." He moved onward with robotic gait.

A couple of months before he had filled in a quiet hour on a journey by reading one of those lurid crime magazines. Somebody had left it on an adjacent seat and he'd picked it up and looked at it out of idle curiosity. One true story therein had told how a dog had unearthed a skeletal hand wearing a plain gold ring, no more than that. From there onward, step by relentless step, tedious lines had been followed, pertinent questions asked, difficult clues developed until eventually the web of entrapment became complete. Sheriffs and their deputies, county attorneys and city detectives scattered right across a continent had picked up jigsaw pieces here and there over a couple of years. Suddenly the total picture had become visible in all its brutal ghastliness—and a man had gone to the electric chair for a crime fourteen years old.

Now there was this. Somewhere within the broad land a scientific bloodhound would be determining the cause of death, the approximate date of the crime, the sex, height, weight and age of the victim plus numerous other details such as only a forensic specialist can extract. The weaving of the web had begun, its completion only a matter of time.

His pulse leaped at the thought of it. How would the end come? At work, at home or perhaps on the way from one to the other? Maybe at home, where he'd hate it most. In a mind stimulated by crisis he could readily imagine the scene. Dorothy would answer the doorbell to admit a couple of burly, grim-faced men and stand wide-eyed while one of them spoke.

"Richard Bransome? We are police officers. We have here a warrant for your arrest and it is our duty to warn you that—"

A scream from Dorothy. The children howling their hearts out and trying to drag him indoors. The pup whining in sympathy and seeking someplace to hide. And the police would take him away, one on each side so that he couldn't run for it. Away from Dorothy, the

26

children, the pup, the home, from everything that he held dear, for ever and ever and ever.

He was perspiring in the coldness of the night when he discovered that he had walked fifty yards past his own house. Swiveling on one heel, he retraced his steps, went up to the front door, and fumbled like a drunk as he sought for his key.

The moment he entered the kids came at him screaming with excitement and trying to climb up his front. Each yell seemed tormentingly shrill, tearing at his nerves in a way never previously experienced. The pup squirmed and wriggled between his feet, making him stumble. He had to put forth a tremendous effort to control himself, blanking his ears to the noises and fixing a thin smile on his face. He scratched two tousled heads, patted two cheeks, stepped carefully over the pup and hung his hat and coat in the hall.

That peculiar perceptiveness of children made them realize that all was not well. They became silent, backing away and regarding him gravely, knowing that he was troubled. He put on a jovial act, but it did not deceive them. In turn, their attitude did nothing to help soothe him inwardly. The very way they looked at him made it seem as if somehow they knew that he was of the doomed.

Dorothy's voice came from the kitchen. "That you, darling? What sort of a day have you had?"

"Worrying," he admitted. Going through to the kitchen, he kissed her and of course gave himself away. He held her a little too tightly and a fraction too long, as if determined never to be deprived of her.

She stood off, studying him, her arched eyebrows crinkled into a frown. "Rich, is it anything serious?"

"Is what serious?"

"Whatever is on your mind."

"Nothing is bothering me particularly," he lied. "Only one or two things at work. I have to go crazy over some problems. It's what I'm paid for."

"Well," she said doubtfully, "don't let them get you down. And don't bring them home with you, either. Home is the place for getting away from all that."

"I know. But worries can't be dismissed that easily.

27

Maybe some people can leave them behind the moment they walk out of the laboratory but I can't. Even at home I need an hour or two to readjust."

"You're not being paid overtime."

"I'm being paid plenty."

"And so you ought," she said, positively. "The best brains deserve the best pay."

He pretended to ruffle her hair. "They get it, my lovely—but there are plenty of brains better than mine."

"Nonsense!" She put a bowl under the mixer and turned a switch. "You're developing an inferiority complex. I'm surprised at you."

"Not so," he contradicted. "A good brain is good enough to recognize a superior one. In the plant are some that must be known to be believed. Clever men, Dorothy, very clever men. I often wish I were as competent."

"Well, if you're not you soon will be."

"I hope so."

He remained there, thinking it over. *Will be,* she had said. The future tense. It might have been valid yesterday. But not today. His future was being taken over by other hands, slowly, piece by piece, damning item after damning item, until someday far or near . . .

"You're unusually quiet this evening. Hungry?"

"Not very."

"Dinner won't be more than a few minutes."

"All right, honey. Just time to wash up."

In the bathroom, he stripped to the waist and washed as if trying to clear away his mental blackness. He was still a little muddle-minded, his brain doing a kind of jittery sideslip each time he bent low over the water.

Dorothy came in hurriedly. "I forgot to tell you there's a fresh towel on the . . . why, Rich, you've bruised your arm."

"Yes, I know." Taking the towel from her, he mopped his face and chest, bent the arm to examine the blue-black patch around the elbow. It felt tender and sore. "Fell down the steps by Branigan's this morning. Banged my elbow and bumped the back of my head."

She felt around his skull, her slim fingers probing his hair. "Yes, there's quite a lump."

"You're telling me. It hurts just to touch it."

"Oh, Rich, you might have broken your neck. Those steps are long. and steep. How on earth did it happen?"

"Not quite sure." He toweled a bit more, reached for his shirt. "I was going down the steps in exactly the same way that I've gone down them hundreds of times. Suddenly I took a dive. Don't remember tripping or slipping. Don't remember feeling ill or fainting or giving way at the knees. I just plunged face-first without warning. Two fellows were mounting the steps and about halfway up. They saw me topple. They jumped forward and grabbed me as I hit. They saved me from serious damage, I guess."

"And then?"

"I must have knocked myself out because I next found myself sitting on the steps in a semi-daze with one of the fellows bending over me and slapping my face and saying, 'Are you all right, mister?' I got to my feet rather shakily, thanked him and went on my way. Needless to say, I felt darned silly."

"Did you see the doctor?"

"No. There wasn't enough reason for doing so. A couple of bumps, that's all I've suffered. I don't rush to the medic and scream for a lollipop every time I bruise myself."

Her gaze went over him with unconcealed anxiety. "But, Rich, if you fainted, as you may have done, it could mean there is something wrong and—"

"There's nothing wrong. I'm fit enough to fall down the Grand Canyon and bounce. Don't get excited about a few bumps and lumps. The kids will be smothered with them before they're through." Finding his shirt, he started replacing it. "I must have been absent-minded or careless and missed my step or something like that. It'll teach me to watch where I'm going. Let's forget it, shall we?"

"All the same, I—" Her voice trailed off, she put on a startled expression. "My goodness, something's burning!" She raced back to the kitchen.

29

He studied himself in the mirror while carefully knotting his tie. Lean, ascetic features, thin lips, dark eyes, black eyebrows and hair. Small white scar on left temple. Clean-shaven. thirtyish, neat dresser in a slightly finicky way. How long before that description became circulated together with details of his finger-prints? How long before some cigar-chewing hack cashed in on him with a yarn entitled *The Phantom Killer of Cooper's Creek* or something like that?

It didn't look like the face of a killer. Too thought-ful and bookish. But it might well fill the part with eyes straining at a police camera and with an identification number hung beneath. Full face and profile, that was the formula. Anyone could look a suit-able candidate for the death-cell when photographed in those circumstances, especially when bleary-eyed and frowsy after a long, long night of intensive question-ing.

"Dinner's ready."

"Coming!" he called.

He didn't really want a meal but would have to go through the motions of eating a hearty one. The alarm permeating his mind was matched by a sickness in his stomach. But abstinence would invite more awkward questions. He'd have to force down the unwanted food as best he could.

"The condemned man ate a four-course breakfast."

Ridiculous!

When facing his imminent end no man could do that.

He passed the security guards shortly before nine in the morning, receiving a nod of recognition from each squad, suffering the usual tedious wait at three succes-sive doors. In theory the guards were supposed to sub-ject his official pass to minute examination each time he went in or came out, even though they had known him for years. This rule had been relaxed after the out-spoken and irascible Cain had erupted when called upon for the seventeenth time to show his document to his own brother-in-law. Now the guards nodded at those well-known and pounced tigerishly upon anyone unrecognized.

Inside, he put his coat and hat in a metal locker,

donned a dark green lab-coat bearing a numbered disk and a radiation-tab, walked along a series of corridors, passed a couple of internal guards and went through a green-painted door. Beyond, he crossed a long, ornate laboratory and several large, imposing workshops, finally reaching a steel shed at the back. This place was the size of an airship hangar. Cain and Potter, both in green lab-coats, were already there, pencils stabbing at drawings scattered along a bench while they discussed some aspect of the thing in the shed's middle.

The shiny, metallic object on the concrete resembled a cross between a huge automobile engine and a long-snouted antiaircraft gun. Its looks were not deceiving. Any competent ballistician could have diagnosed its purpose after brief examination. A small row of missiles standing by its base were a dead giveaway: proximity-fuzed shells without propulsive charges.

The subject of the Cain-Potter discussion was an experimental model of a fully automatic high-angle gun made especially spiteful by use of a new liquid explosive. The latter could be pumped, carbureted, injected and fired electrically. On the drawing-board this gadget was capable of throwing six hundred heavy-caliber shells per minute to an altitude of seventy thousand feet. But on the test range it had proved a different story altogether: within eight seconds missiles had been wobbling wildly upward from a barrel worn and expanded by frictional heat.

So they had tried various modifications that had gained them a mere four seconds of effective fire. The basic idea was first-class but in actual practice more full of bugs than a flea-trainer's dog. If weeks or months of trial and error, argument and head-beating could create perfection they'd have had a gadget capable of tearing the skies apart.

Right now they had reached the stage of eating their nails while seeking a solution to the problem of how to reduce the rate of fire without actually reducing the rate of fire. This was not as impossible as it might seem; at the last resort they could substitute a multi-barreled gun designed to fire in series. But they were not yet ready for the last resort.

Cain ceased yabbering at Potter, turned to Bran-

31

some and said, "Here's another frustrated genius. For your information we have come to an unavoidable conclusion."

"And what is that?" asked Bransome.

"Either the barrel lining or the shells must be made of frictionless alloy," responded Cain, giving a lopsided grin. "As an allegedly expert metallurgist it's your job to invent it. So go ahead and get busy."

"Be nice if I could."

"They're riding Hilderman," put in Potter. "If his department can stabilize this bang-stuff the way they want"—he gestured toward the gun—"we can sling this piece of junk into the river. The missiles will be self-propelled and all we'll need to build will be a great grand-daddy of a belt-fed, radar-controlled bazooka."

"Not being in the explosives line I don't know what's wrong with it for that purpose," said Cain. "You can bet it's been given a trial and found wanting in some important respect." He walked four times around the gun, then complained loudly, "This thing is the victim of its own efficiency. We've got to find some way of cutting out the grief while retaining all the pleasure. Why don't I become a bookie and take life easier?"

"It'll have to be multi-barrels," observed Potter.

"Only as an admission of defeat. I refuse to admit defeat and so do you. No surrender. *Ils ne passeront pas.* I helped build this ugly futility. It's my life. It's my love. Criticism be damned." He sought sentimental support from Bransome. "Would *you* destroy the object of your affection merely because she was giving trouble?" Then he watched Bransome turn white and walk away without answering. After a few pregnant moments he turned to Potter and asked in surprised tones, "What did I say wrong? Hell's bells, I couldn't tell if he was going to kill me or jump through the window. I've never known him to behave like that before. What did I say wrong?"

Potter stared at the door through which Bransome had gone and hazarded, "You must have trampled on one of his pet corns."

"What corn? All I said was—"

"I know what you said. I heard it with both ears. Evidently it meant something to him, something special

32

and touchy. Perhaps he's having trouble at home. Maybe he and his wife have had a battle and he's invited her to drop dead."

"He'd never do that. I know him pretty well. He's not the kind to play-act in a domestic drama and emote all over the house."

"His wife may be. Some women can work themselves up into a state of hysteria over nothing at all. What if his wife is making things unbearable for him?"

"My guess is that he'd keep his mouth firmly shut and refuse to add fuel to the flames. If in spite of that she pushed him too far he'd quietly pack his bags and walk out for keeps."

"Yes, that's how I weigh him up," agreed Potter. "But we could be wrong. No man really knows what another might do in a major crisis. Every disaster brings the most unexpected reactions. The big, tough, loud-mouthed types dive into foxholes while some quiet and weedy little guy does something heroic."

"To blazes with him, anyway," said Cain, impatiently. "Let him solve his own problems while we try to get a grip on ours."

Moving to the drawings on the bench, they considered them afresh.

THREE:

BRANSOME LEFT at five, exchanged nods with the
guards and started home. It had been a bad day, the
lousiest day he could recall. Everything had gone
wrong, nothing right. He seemed to have spent a large
part of his time looking over his shoulder, beating
away his fears and making unsatisfactory attempts to
concentrate on his work.

Ability to concentrate is the prime virtue in any
scientific research establishment. How can a man do it
with a death-cell depicted in his mind? Up to now he
had suffered approximately twenty-four hours of nervous strain merely because a couple of truck-drivers had
gossiped about an unknown crime at some unspecified
place near Burleston. The tree they had discussed was
not necessarily *his* tree, the bones not necessarily those
of *his* victim. It might be that belatedly somebody else's
misdeed had been brought to light. Right now the hunt
might be in full cry after some other quarry.

A pity, he thought, that he hadn't had the gumption
to join the truckers' conversation and steer it deftly
around until he got the details he needed to know.
Would that have been wise? Yes—if their information
had proved of a nature calming to his fears. No—if it
confirmed his worst apprehensions. And in the latter
case his interest might arouse suspicion. The grouchy
trucker who had been personally involved might display a dangerous shrewdness.

"Say, what's this to you, mister?"

How could he answer? What could he say? Only
something silly and unconvincing that might invite further trouble.

"Oh, I once lived around those parts."

"Did you now? Burleston, eh? Do you remember a

woman disappearing in that locality? Or can you name anyone who might recall it? Maybe *you* know something about this, huh?"

If those two were in the snack bar again this evening would it be best to ignore them or would it pay to join them and entice them to talk in a more revealing way? For the life of him he couldn't decide.

These considerations fled from his mind when he turned a corner and found a cop standing there. His pulse gave a jump. He walked past trying desperately to look casual and unconcerned, even pursing his lips in a silent, carefree whistle.

The cop's eyes bored at him, glittering in the shadow beneath the visor of his cap. Bransome paced steadily on, feeling or imagining that he could feel the other's stare burning into the back of his neck. He wondered whether he had drawn attention to himself by overdoing the indifference, much as a naughty child betrays himself by exaggerated innocence.

Moving onward with nerves drawn taut, he knew that a sudden, authoritative bellow of, "Hey, you!" would get him on the run. He'd race like mad across streets, through traffic, along back alleys, with feet pounding after him and whistles blowing and people shouting. He'd run and run and run until he dropped exhausted. And then they'd take him.

No shout sounded to start him off. Reaching the next corner he could not resist taking a wary glance behind. The cop was still there and still gazing toward him. Rounding the corner, Bransome counted a slow ten, had another look back. The cop was in the same place but his attention was now turned the opposite way.

Sweating with relief, he continued to the station. There he bought an evening paper, sought hurriedly through it for any item of news vital to him, failed to find one. But that meant nothing. The police give reporters a handout only when it suits them and not before; often it does not suit them until they're able to name the culprit and invite the press to aid the hunt.

His train rolled in and carried him to the junction. Dismounting, he went to the snack bar. The two truckers were not there. He didn't know whether to feel relieved or disappointed. The only other customer was a huge, blank-faced man sitting astride a high stool and gazing boredly at the mirror back of the counter.

Ordering black coffee, Bransome sipped and after a while met the big man's eyes in the mirror. It seemed to him that the other was not idly glancing at him but rather examining him with more than usual interest. Bransome looked away, let a minute go past and then looked back. The big man was still watching him in the mirror and making no effort to conceal the fact. He had a kind of massive arrogance as if in the habit of staring at people and openly challenging them to do something about it.

A railroad worker came in, bought two wrapped sandwiches and took them out. The big man remained firmly on his stool and kept his inquisitive gaze fixed on the mirror. Drinking his coffee with studied unconcern, Bransome tried hard to avoid looking at the mirror but his attention kept drifting back to it as if drawn there by a form of hypnosis. Every time he met the other eye to eye.

I'll have to avoid this place, he decided. Been coming here too regularly and too long. Set up an unbroken routine and the pursuers know exactly where to look for you. All they need do is go sniffing along your self-created rut and pick you up at one end or the other. Destroy the routine and they no longer know where in hell you are.

"They"?

Who are "they"?

The various officers of the law, of course. This bull-sized starer could be just such a one. Yes, that was a definite possibility. He could be a cop in plain clothes, lacking enough evidence to justify an immediate arrest but hoping that guilt could be made to ferment like yeast so that he, Bransome, would get the jitters and betray himself in some fatal manner.

Well, he wasn't going to betray himself, not while he remained in full possession of his senses. The police had found a collection of human bones and they were welcome to handle the resulting problem without any help from him. So far as he was concerned he'd give them a gallop for their money—because life is sweet even with

36

a major burden on the mind and death is full of terror no matter how deserved.

Leaving his drink unfinished he edged off his stool and walked to the door. The big man twisted around and slowly came to his feet, his full attention on the other. His manner was that of one giving the quarry a slight lead merely for the fun of it; a professional pursuer unable to relish the chase when capture became too easy.

If the idea was to make Bransome bolt like a startled rabbit, it didn't work. Though the rawest of amateurs at this game of evading the law, Bransome was no dope. He was a man of high I.Q. trying to deal with a situation all too familiar to members of the underworld but quite strange to himself. He was willing to learn and slowly but surely was learning. One petty scare over that uniformed cop earlier had taught him not to react too swiftly or too openly. Everyone chases an obvious fugitive.

The correct concealing tactic, he decided, is to behave normally when one is feeling far from normal, to maintain an unswerving pretense that one is an insignificant part of humanity when one is beyond the pale of it. That is hard, terribly hard, when one has had no training as an actor, no conditioning in deceit, and bears in his skull a brain that tends to keep sounding shrill warnings like an intermittent alarm clock. But it had to be done.

So as he went out he forced himself to give the big man stare for stare. Reaching the station's departure track, he boarded his train, getting into the rearmost car. This gave him a vantage point from which he could watch later comers while pretending to read his paper.

He sat tensely, looking over the top edge of the paper, until he saw the big man lumber down the platform and board the train a couple of cars nearer the front. That was the car that he, Bransome, usually occupied, the one in which Connelly and Farmiloe would now be seated.

Why had the big man picked on that particular car? Was it sheer coincidence or was he betting on the quarry's known habits? In the latter event he was likely to do something about it when he discovered that Bransome was not among those present. Just what would he do? Obviously he'd be in something of a quandary since there would not be enough time to explore the entire train before it departed. He'd have to make his choice between staying on the train and searching it or getting off to snoop around the station.

The train hooted, gave a slight jerk, trundled forward with gathering speed, clanked over switches and sped onward. There was no evidence that the big man had gotten off. He must have remained aboard. If he stayed put and did not get off at Bransome's station, all would be well. The brief series of events would serve to show that a guilty mind can be suspicious of a stray cat.

But if the big man took a walk along the train's aisle or maintained a watch at various stops and got off with Bransome . . .

Perhaps even now he was engaging Connelly and Farmiloe in conversation, cunningly steering the talk the way he wanted it to go, prying out items of information that meant nothing to the tellers but plenty to the listener, doing it with the disarming dexterousness of the professional snooper. Maybe he would learn that this was the first evening in months that Bransome had failed to travel with the pair of them, that yesterday evening his manner had been strange, that he had been preoccupied and ill-at-ease and so on.

This kind of thing brought another dilemma to the hunted. Stay in a rut and one is tracked; jump out of it and one immediately attracts attention. Behave with absolute normality and one can be followed along his chosen path of habitude; break away from the path and one is harder to find but more surely wanted.

"Innocent, are you? Then why did you take pains to give us the runaround?"

Or, "We had a to chase you. Only the guilty-minded give us a chase. Talk your way out of that."

And they'd take it from there.

"Why did you kill Arline?"

"Come on now, quit this horsing around. Tell us all you know about Arline . . . Arline—"

It hit him like a brick.
Arline *who?*

The train rolled into his station and stopped. He got off automatically, without being fully aware of what he was doing. He was so occupied with the puzzle of his victim's surname that he quite forgot to look for the big man.

"Surely I should know the identity of the woman I buried? I may have become fuzzy-minded—but not to that extent. The name must be located at the back of my brain but for some reason I can't bring it forward. Twenty years is a long time. I know I tried hard to expunge that episode from my memory, to treat it as something that never really happened, a bad but meaningless dream. Yet it's strange that I cannot recall her family name."

Arline—?"

The big man hove enormously into view as the train gave a raucous hoot and moved on. The name-problem promptly fled from Bransome's mind as he passed through the exit and walked steadily along the approach road. There was a coldness in his back hairs as he heard the slow, deliberate tread of the other's feet a mere twenty paces behind.

He turned a corner. So did the other. He crossed the street. So did the other. He entered his own street and the big man followed suit.

Problems were piling upon problems. Now he had a new one. Question: did the big man know his address or was he following for the purpose of discovering it? In the former case Bransome might just as well walk boldly into his own home. In the latter case to do so would be to provide needed information.

Reaching a decision, he tramped right past his house and frantically hoped that the kids would not see him and rush out yelling and thus reveal what he preferred to conceal. Not for a moment did it occur to him to wonder why a shadower should make so careless a job of his shadowing. If he had given the matter any consideration he'd have concluded that the purpose was to make him panic and that the shadower was functioning as a stimulator of self-betrayal.

No familiar figure endangered his walk-onward tactic until young Jimmy Lindstrom came round the top corner. Bransome immediately avoided an encounter by turning down a side street. The heavy footsteps faithfully followed.

At the other end of this street a cop was lounging under a lamp. The sight of him made Bransome hesitate for a moment. Then it struck him that here was a situation where boldness might pay.

Speeding up his pace, he reached the cop and said, "A big fellow has been following me for most of half an hour. I don't like it. He may be after my wallet."

"Which fellow?" asked the other, peering along the street.

Bransome looked back. The subject of his complaint was nowhere to be seen.

"He was right behind me as far as the last corner. I heard him turn it."

The cop sucked at his teeth and suggested, "Let's go back there."

He accompanied Bransome to the corner. There was no sign of the shadower.

"You sure you didn't imagine him?"

"I'm positive," said Bransome, feeling foolish.

"Then he must have gone into a house or dived down an alley," the cop decided. "If he did enter a house, well, you've nothing to worry about. He followed you because he uses the same way home."

"Could be. But I know most of the folks around here. He was a complete stranger."

"That means nothing," scoffed the cop. "People come and go all the time. If I got the jumps every time I saw a new face I'd have been white-haired ten years ago." He studied Bransome curiously. "Are you carrying a big wad or something?"

"No, I'm not."

"Where d'you live?"

"Just over there," said Bransome, pointing.

"All right, mister. You go home and take it easy. I'll be watching and I'll be around for quite a piece."

"Thanks," said Bransome. "Sorry to have troubled you."

He headed for home, inwardly wondering whether he

had done the right thing. For all he knew he might still be within observation of the big man who, because of the cop, had become more discreet. True, the suspected shadower might be an innocent newcomer to the locality, but if he were not . . .

This business of being on the run, mentally at any rate, was like playing superfast chess with his own life as the stake. A false move here and another there and the game inevitably must lead to checkmate. It seemed to him incredible that other wanted men could endure such a situation for months, even for years before they gained psychological relief by giving themselves up. The intensity of the strain, he felt, was a feature that most men could handle—but the prolongation was something else again.

For the first time he began to speculate about the question of just how long he would last and in what manner he would precipitate the dreaded end.

Dorothy said with wifely concern, "Why, Rich, your face is flushed and hot. And on a cool evening like this."

He kissed her. "I've been hurrying. Don't know why. Just felt I wanted to put a move on"

"Hurrying?" She frowned in bafflement and glanced. at the clock. "But you're a few minutes later than usual. Was the train late?"

He bit back an affirmative before it could pop out. So easy to tell lies and so easy to be found out. Problems still were piling up. Now he was being tempted to deceive his own wife. Even in such a minor matter as this he couldn't do it and wouldn't do it—or not yet.

"No, dear, I wasted a bit of time talking to a cop."

"That needn't have made you race like mad. Dinner can wait a while, you know that." She put a slender hand on his cheek. "Rich, are you telling me the truth?"

"The truth about what?"

"About yourself. Are you sure you feel all right?"

"Of course I'm all right. I feel topnotch."

"Not a little bit headachy or feverish?"

"Why on earth do you ask me that?" he demanded.

"You're flushed, as I've told you. And you're not your usual self. I can sense it every time. I've lived with

41

you long enough to know when you're down in the dumps."

"Oh, stop picking on me!" he snapped. He felt contrite immediately and added, "Sorry, Honey, I've had a tough day. I'll go wash and freshen up."

He went to the bathroom, his mind brooding over the knowledge that all this had happened before. A nervy homecoming, awkward questions from Dorothy, evasions on his part, flight to the bathroom. It couldn't go on evening after evening, week after week—assuming that he remained free for any length of time. And there were doubts about that.

Stripping to the waist, he examined his elbow. It still bore a blue-black patch and felt a little stiff but was less sore. The bump on his head had gone down considerably; when he'd taken that tumble he couldn't have hit so hard after all.

In a short time he joined the family for dinner. They sat around the table and ate in unaccustomed silence. Even the pup was subdued. Over the house lay a dark shadow that all could sense but none could see. After a while the strain became too much. They broke the silence with brief remarks and equally short responses. But that conversation was forced and artificial and they knew it.

In bed that night Dorothy lay restlessly for most of an hour, turning first to one side and then the other, before she whispered, "Rich, are you awake?"

"Yes," he admitted, knowing that he could not fool her by pretending to be asleep.

"How about taking a week off from work?"

"My vacation isn't due just yet."

"Couldn't you ask them for a week in advance?"

"Why?"

"You need the break. It would do you good."

"Now look here—" He stopped, choking off his irritation as an idea struck him. Then he finished, "I'll see how I feel about it in the morning. Let's try to get to sleep now, shall we? It's late enough already."

Her hand reached out and patted his.

Over breakfast she renewed the subject. "Grab yourself a spell of time off, Rich. Others do it often enough, whenever they feel wound up. Why shouldn't you? You're not the only original Cast Iron Man."

"I'm not wound up either."

"I don't want you to be. A well-earned rest could make all the difference."

"Difference between what?" he asked.

"Having and not having something to worry about," she gave back. "I know your job means a lot to you but it isn't everything. Health comes first."

"Nobody's ever been killed by work."

"That's exactly what Jeff Anderson told his wife, remember?"

He winced and said, "Jeff's stroke wasn't necessarily brought on by overwork. It was just one of those things."

"Maybe it was," she admitted. "And maybe it wasn't."

"Listen who's talking," he said, jocularly. "You accuse me of worrying too much but you're doing plenty yourself."

"Rich, we're married. We're supposed to consider each other. If we don't, who will?"

"All right." He left the table, found his hat and briefcase, kissed her near the front door. "I'll think it over on the train.

With that, he departed.

He stuck it out for four more days, fending off the curious and the querulous at work, fighting a delaying action with Dorothy each night. On the first evening the big man followed him home again. The other three evenings he switched routes and lost the unwelcome tracker.. Since each route was longer and consumed more time, he got home late. That meant more innocent questions from Dorothy, more evasions that served only to add to her uneasiness. He could see that Dorothy's worry was growing and that she was doing her best to conceal the fact.

At work the going was rough. In spite of all his efforts to appear perfectly normal his subtle change of character was evident to colleagues on familiar terms with him..His sudden lapses leading to minor blunders,

43

his occasional moments of being slow on the uptake, caused confreres to look at him askance. A few addressed him with unusual solicitude, in the manner of men concerned for the sick or soon to be sick.

The fourth day was by far the worst. A tall, sharp-eyed, loose-limbed character named Reardon appeared in the plant and hung around the green area most of the time, especially those parts near where Bransome was working. Bransome's abnormal sensitivity told him that this newcomer was keeping watch upon him though at no time could he catch him doing so openly. But since nobody could roam the plant witout the backing of top authority, it meant that the snooping must have official approval.

Surely the hunters couldn't have picked up the trail so swiftly, after twenty long, long years? Could it be that already they had managed to identify the culprit and were keeping him under constant surveillance pending production of enough evidence to provide legal proof? The matter preyed so much on his mind that he couldn't resist sounding Potter on the subject during the lunch break.

"Who's this Reardon fellow who seems able to live without working?"

"Some kind of investigator, I think."

"That so? Who or what is he supposed to be investigating?"

"Darned if I know," said Potter, little caring. "I've seen him around before, some time back. About eighteen months ago."

"He wasn't in our area. I've never set eyes on him in my life until recently."

"He was loafing around in the red area," asserted Potter, "so you might not have noticed him. He arrived soon after Henderson took off. Everyone thought he was Henderson's replacement but he wasn't. He just hung around for a couple of weeks, doing nothing and saying nothing, then went back to wherever he came from. Maybe his job is to tour all the defense plants and make sure nobody is wasting time shooting craps. Maybe somebody in Washington thinks we'd all become incurable crap-shooters unless a beady eye is put upon us from time to time."

"Some investigator," opined Bransome doubtfully. "Meanders all over the place chain-smoking and voicing not a word. Never asks any questions."

"You want questions?"

"No."

"Then what are you griping about?"

"It gives me the fidgets to have some snooper breathing down my neck."

"Doesn't bother me," said Potter, radiating virtue. "I've got a clear conscience."

Bransome stared hard at him, firmed his lips, and that was the end of the conversation.

He knew he could not stand another day of this, with remarks like Potter's jolting his brain, with Reardon's sharp, inquisitive gaze always near at hand, with the big man to be avoided on the way home and Dorothy to be faced each evening and night. A desperate resolve mounted within him: the time had come to make a break.

When work ceased he went straight to the personnel office, found Markham and said, "I hate to come at you without warning but I'd like to take a week off, without pay, starting tomorrow."

"Why without pay?"

"I don't want to cut into my vacation time."

Markham registered sympathy. "Trouble at home? Kids ill or something?"

"No, nothing like that." He sought around for a plausible pretext. It seemed as if he were doomed to spend the rest of his years mouthing deceptions, finding excuses, seeking pretexts. "It's a difficulty with relatives. I'd like to go visiting some distance away and try to clear matters up."

"This is rather irregular," said Markham, pursing his lips.

"I know. I wouldn't ask if it weren't imperative."

"I'm sure you wouldn't." He pondered a moment, picked up the phone, switched through to Cain and chatted briefly. Then he said to Bransome, "Cain doesn't object and that means Laidler can't object, either. It's all right with me. You'll be back a week from tomorrow?"

"Yes."

"Okay. I'll have it noted on your card."

"Thanks a lot. I appreciate it."

He went out just as Reardon came in. A sidewise glance as he passed the window showed Reardon talking to Markham. For some reason he quickened his pace.

A casual acquaintance who happened to be going his way gave him a lift in an asthmatic car and took him most of the way home. That enabled him to evade the big man again and arrive on time. Perhaps his luck was about to change. He had come to the state of imagining things a lot better when they ceased to grow worse.

The family responded with alacrity to his slight perking up. It showed how deeply they must have been affected by his gloom. The kids shrilled, the pup gyrated and wet the carpet. Dorothy smiled, glanced at the clock and bustled around the kitchen.

"I'm going away, Honey."

She paused, saucepan in hand. "You mean you're taking a holiday as I suggested?"

"Of course not. I wouldn't snatch a vacation all by myself, without you and the kids. That wouldn't be a holiday at all. This is the next best thing."

"What is it then?"

"I'm going on business, just for a week. It'll be quite a change and as good as a rest."

"I'm glad to hear it. That's just what you need." She put down the pan and capped it with a lid. "Where are they sending you, dear?"

Where?

Up to this moment he hadn't thought of it, not even for the purpose of having a ready reply. All that had been in his mind was to get away from here and from the plant, away to some place devoid of trackers and questioners, a temporary hideout where he could sit in peace, review his predicament and try to concoct a satisfactory solution.

Where?

She was awaiting his reply and becoming conscious of the delay.

"Burleston," he said. He did not know why he said

46

it. The hated name popped out of his mouth of its own accord.

"Where's that?"

"It's a small place in the Midwest."

"Oh, is it? Why—"

He continued hurriedly to stall further questions, knowing the most natural one would be what state Burleston was in. "I'll be there only two or three days. I don't plan to fly. I'll go by train, lolling back in my seat and enjoying the scenery. Just a lazy bum." He forced a grin and hoped it looked convincing. "The trip will be boring, all by myself. Wish you could come along."

"What, and leave the children to themselves? Or take them away from school for a week? Don't be silly!" She carried on with kitchen work, her spirits visibly improved. "You make the most of your trip to Burleston, Rich. Eat well, sleep well and don't worry about anything. You'll come back fighting fit."

"Yes, Doctor," he said, showing false meekness.

Come back to what? There was only the dangerous rut to which he could return. Obviously it would be a waste of time to jump out of it unless he could stay out.

So within this coming week he must, if possible, find a new, anonymous life some place where official eyes would not watch his every move, where feet would not follow in the steps of his own. It would not be enough merely to achieve that much: he must also devise a method of spiriting Dorothy and the children out of one home and into another, suddenly and without trace. To do that he would have to give Dorothy the facts so far denied to her but that prospect could be faced after other problems had been solved—if it were possible to find a complete solution.

One alternative was to abandon his family and thus deprive searchers of a point of contact.

He could not do that, risky though it might be to cling to them. He would not do it unless forced by circumstances utterly beyond his control.

Sentence of death would be such a circumstance.

47

FOUR:

IN THE morning he left home by taxi, taking one suit-case and traveling light. Dorothy stood in the drive-way by the family car, smiling goodbye and making ready to take the children to school. The kids jigged up and down upon the lawn and waved him away. It oc-curred to him with a touch of panic that if he were picked up during the next few days this might well be the last time he'd ever see them thus. Peering through the cab's rear window he drank in the view until a cor-ner cut them off from sight.

The cab made a brief stop at the local bank while he withdrew a modest sum. A larger amount would make things easier for him but harder for Dorothy if events proved against their earlier reunion. He had to strike a compromise between his immediate needs and her fu-ture ones. They had saved assiduously without piling up enough to splurge.

From there he went to the station. The cab rolled away and left him warily seeking familiar faces. There weren't any around just then, for which he was pro-foundly thankful. He was going to town an hour later than usual and that saved him from the inquisitiveness of fellow commuters.

The train took him away. He arrived in town with-out untoward incident, and became as lost in scurrying millions as a grain in a truckload of sand. There was no plan in his mind other than that of ridding himself of all followers while he sought a means of coping with his woes. He had the vague idea that the past cannot easily catch up with one who moves around, therefore the essential thing was to keep moving, erratically, without foreseeable system.

More or less aimlessly he tramped along crowded

48

sidewalks, his suitcase hanging at his side, until suddenly he found himself at the main-line station. Then and only then did he realize that some independent and unhampered portion of his mind had steered him here, having decided his route from the start. It seemed strange, he thought, that a confused and apprehensive brain could retain a small section capable of calm thought and ready command. Since he was little given to self-examination it did not occur to him that a basically emotional problem can swirl over but never drown a basically analytical mind.

Anyway, he obeyed the inward order or instinct or whatever it was. Entering the station he went to a ticket window and gazed owl-eyed at the clerk as it dawned upon him that he must now declare his destination. One could not ask for a ticket to somewhere safe, beyond reach of the law. One must name a place of one's choice, any place, even the first one that comes to mind. Indeed, his mouth opened to form the word but he bit it back in the nick of time: the same word he had voiced to Dorothy when called upon to answer without thinking.

The other portion of his mind, the part remaining craftily alert, held the word back. If they come looking for you, it argued, they'll trace you to town and rake the train and bus stations for someone who remembers the item they wish to learn. They'll talk to this clerk visit—and say too much. Don't take a chance on him. hundreds of people per day he may have an excellent memory and find some obscure reason to recall your visit—and say too much. Don't take a chance on him. Don't take a chance on *anyone*. All the characters rotting in jails are the stupid ones who accepted unnecessary risks.

Bransome bought a ticket to a big city three-quarters of the way to where he really wanted to go. Pocketing the ticket, he picked up his case, turned around and almost bumped into a tall, lean man with crew-cut hair and gimlet eyes.

"Well now, Mr. Bransome," said Reardon pleasantly but showing no great surprise. "Giving yourself a vacation?"

"With official permission," informed Bransome,

49

making a gigantic effort to control himself. "People do take time off once in a while."

"Of course," approved Reardon. "Sure they do." He looked with pointed interest at the other's case, his air being that of one able to see right inside anything at which he gazed. "Have yourself a good time."

"That is my intention." Then resentment sparked and Bransome demanded, "What are you doing here, anyway?"

"The same as yourself." Reardon gave a half-smile. "I'm going somewhere. We wouldn't happen to be going the same way, would we?"

"I've no idea," Bransome riposted, "not knowing your destination."

"Oh, well, what does it matter?" said Reardon, refusing to bite. He eyed the station clock, edged toward the ticket window. "Have to hurry. Be seeing you sometime."

"Maybe," said Bransome, showing no ecstasy at the prospect.

He made for his train, relieved and yet not relieved at getting rid of Reardon. His mind was jumpier than a cat at a fireworks display. Meeting the fellow here seemed too much for coincidence. He had a swift, wary look around as he passed through the gates. There was no sign of Reardon at that moment.

Ten minutes passed before the train pulled out; he spent the time edgily expecting unwanted company. If Reardon were trailing him and had documentary authority to prove his right to twist the arm of the ticket clerk, it would be easy for him to demand a ticket as issued to the previous buyer and board the same train. The last thing Bransome wanted was the snoop's face on the opposite seat, with several hours of conversation to be handled cagily, endless pointed remarks and penetrating questions to be fended off. He kept anxious watch through the window but eventually the train moved out with nothing to show that Reardon had caught it.

Reaching the terminal after an uneventful trip, Bransome walked haphazardly around the city and kept surreptitious watch behind him but failed to spot a follower of any kind. He treated himself to an indifferent meal, mooched about a little longer and returned to the station. So far as he could tell nobody had tracked him thus far and nobody was hanging around the station entrance in expectation of his reappearance.

At the ticket window he said, "I want to get to Burleston."

"No rail service to that place," replied the clerk. "Nearest station is Hanbury, twenty-four miles away. A bus will take you from Hanbury to Burleston."

"All right. Fix me up for Hanbury. What time is the next train?"

"You're in luck. Two minutes from now. Track Nine —and you'd better hustle."

Grabbing his ticket, Bransome galloped across the waiting room and through the gate to Track Nine. He made it nicely; the train started to move before he was settled in his seat. That gave him much satisfaction; he felt that the speed of his departure must have shaken off pursuit if indeed he really was being pursued.

Here was the curse of being burdened with a past dragged willy-nilly into the present and making the present equally grim: the constant, unshakable, never-ending sensation of being watched, suspected, followed. The obsession of being surrounded by eyes that stared and saw the truth and accused.

Why did I kill Arline?

There was a faint queasiness in his stomach as he pondered the question. For some elusive reason the details came back more clearly now that he was less preoccupied with immediate dangers.

He could remember her surname now, Arline Lafarge, yes, that had been her name. She had once explained to him that her first name was another version of Eileen and that the last was attributable to French ancestry. She'd had a wonderful figure to which she'd given every possible emphasis and that was as much as could be said for her. In other respects she'd been black-haired, black-eyed, completely calculating and completely callous, an old witch in youthful guise if ever there was one.

She had gained an almost hypnotic hold over him

51

when he was not quite twenty and must have been a ten times bigger fool than he'd ever been before or since. She'd announced her intention of exploiting her control to the utmost just as soon as he became fit for use, by which she meant she was biding her time until he left college, found a job and started making good money. Meanwhile, he was to be her willing love-slave, waiting and yearning for the ultimate reward of her body. Every once in a while she wanted reassurance that her hold remained good and tight. Dutifully he had put on the required lap-dog acts, wanting her and hating her at one and the same time.

So then two decades back had come the explosion. She had summoned him to Burleston just for a day, wanting to dangle the bait just beyond reach of the poor fish, wanting to gloat over him, wipe her feet on him, satisfy herself for the twelfth or twentieth time that he was wholly hers, body and soul.

That had been her mistake, to call him just then. He'd had enough and more than enough of this junior Cleopatra. Something had snapped, his liver had taken over from his heart, and his hatred had built up to critical mass. He could have thrown her over if his fury had not been too great to be satisfied with this simple solution. So he had gone to Burleston and bashed her skull in. Then he had buried her under a tree.

He must have been crazy.

The details of that act now shone vividly in his imagination as if embossed thereon a few days ago rather than twenty years back. He could see her pale oval face as she collapsed beneath a vicious blow, her crumpled form lying still, unmoving, a thin trickle of blood creeping from the edge of her black hair and matching the blood-red of her lips. He could still sense the insane violence with which he had struck and even as he thought of it his arm tensed as if in readiness to strike again. He could recall with complete clarity the frantic energy with which he had scrabbled a burrow large enough to hold the body, meanwhile watching the lonely road for any oncomer who might catch him in the act. He could see himself carefully replacing the last torn-up clods between the tree's roots and trampling them firm to conceal all signs of disturbance.

52

And then had followed a long period of mental training designed to protect him from the past; a stringent form of self-discipline by means of which he had almost convinced himself that the deed never had been done, Arline Lafarge had never existed, never in his life had he been in or near Burleston.

To some extent he must have succeeded in expunging evil memories as the years rolled by. Today his crime could be pictured in sharp focus and full color but on preceding and subsequent events he was decidedly hazy. It had taken quite a time to remember that Arline's name had been Lafarge. Try as he might he could not bring the township of Burleston to mind with any accuracy; in fact, his efforts to recall its scenes left him unsure whether he was resurrecting the correct ones or confusing them with some other small place visited in the long ago. In the past he had traveled around quite a lot and had seen plenty of one-horse country towns; at this date it wasn't easy to sort out one from another. And another thing: right now he couldn't imagine why Arline had gone to Burleston in the first place.

Above all, he could not for the life of him recall the precise nature of Arline's hold over him. Obviously he should be able to remember it because therein lay the basic motivation of his crime. Yet he could not. Even if one made full allowance for the desires and emotions of youth, mere detestation was not enough—or not enough for a man of his thoughtful type. So far as his possibly inhibited memory went, he had not committed more than his share of youthful follies, had never been known as a wildcat. There must have been a better-than-average reason for ridding himself of Arline. Somewhere at some time he must have done something that could effectively have ruined his career if found out, something that Arline had known about and held over him.

But he had not the slightest recollection of it. What had it been? A theft? An armed robbery? An embezzlement or a forgery? In his imagination he went through the details of his life from babyhood to the twenties and failed to dig out a single deed of enough consequence to place him at the mercy of a scheming female.

So far as his memory could be trusted his only delinquencies had been childish ones such as blacking the eye of a mother's pet or breaking a window with a ball. No more than that.

Wearily he rubbed his forehead, knowing that intense nervous strain can play hob with rational thought, wondering whether any of the bright brains with whom he worked ever became afflicted with a similar mental hiatus. Once or twice he also speculated rather fearfully about his own mental condition. Was he really normal or was it that some latent abnormality—first evident twenty years ago—was now reasserting itself in readiness to develop into a certifiable condition? He may have been a little mad *then*—he might not be as sane as he believed *now*.

Darkness had fallen by the time he reached Hanbury. He took a room at a small hotel, slept erratically with many tossings and turnings, breakfasted heavy-eyed and without appetite. The first bus to Burleston left at nine-thirty. He caught it, leaving his suitcase at the hotel.

The bus got him there at ten-fifteen. Dismounting, he stared up and down the street, entirely failing to recognize it. This did not mystify him. Places can and do change a lot in twenty years. Sometimes they alter out of all semblance to their original form as old buildings are knocked down, new ones take their places, vacant lots become occupied, garbage dumps are cleared away. In twenty years a hamlet can become a village, a village can grow into a town and a town into a city.

To the best of his judgment Burleston was now a small country town of about four thousand population. It was bigger than he'd expected. He knew of no reason why he had imagined it smaller except, perhaps, that a memory of his last visit was lodged somewhere in his subconscious.

For some time he stood in the street uncertain what to do next. He hadn't the vaguest notion why flight from inward fears had brought him to this place, only that he had obeyed an instinct seemingly without rhyme or reason. Perhaps it was the much-vaunted desire of the criminal to return to the scene of his crime.

54

It could be, in fact it was likely to be, because he felt very much impelled to visit the actual scene—without knowing if it were north, south, east or west of his present position.

His memory supplied only the vision of a length of country road no different from a thousand other roads. In his mind's eye he could see that stretch vividly enough: a straight two-lane highway, smoothly macadamed, with young trees lining the shoulders at fifty-foot intervals. Fields around full of corn standing knee-high. One tree in particular, the one under which he had dug a tunnel down below the spreading roots. He had shoved her into it head-first. Her shoes had peeped out before he'd hidden them with the last of the earth and reset the lumps of coarse grass.

Somewhere outside of Burleston it had been, must have been. A mile beyond the outskirts, five miles, ten? He did not know. And in which direction? He didn't know that, either. In this street were no familiar pointers, nothing to give him a clue.

Eventually he dealt with the problem in a manner best calculated to avoid the questions of the curious. Hiring a taxi, he told the driver that he was a business executive seeking a site for a small factory outside of town. The driver, accepting him at face value, took him on a comprehensive tour of all roads within ten miles of Burleston. It was a dead loss. At no point did they pass a scene that the passenger could recognize.

When they got back to their starting point, Bransome said to the driver, "I've been tipped to look at a cornfield alongside a two-lane road. The road has trees planted at regular intervals along the sides. Know where that might be?"

"No, chief. You've been along every route outside of this town. There ain't any more. I don't know of any tree-lined road nearer than ten miles the other side of Hanbury. Take you there if you want."

"No, thanks," said Bransome, hurriedly. "The advice I was given definitely said Burleston."

"Then somebody got it wrong," asserted the driver. "Wise guys usually get it wrong." With that piece of philosophy he drove away.

Well, perhaps the road had been widened and its

trees cut down. Perhaps he had ridden within a few yards of the fateful spot without knowing it. But no, that wasn't likely. The gabby trucker who had scared him in the first place had talked about a tree leaning over the road and near to falling. That one, at least, could not have been cut at the time. It was a good guess that all the other trees were still there—unless cut very recently. But he had seen no evidence of roadside felling during his ride in the taxi.

Restlessly he walked several times up and down the main street, looking at shops, stores, taverns and service stations, hoping to stimulate his memory and get himself a clue of some kind, any kind. It was to no avail. The whole place remained as completely strange as any unknown town. If in fact it were an unknown town, if indeed he had never been here before, he must have got the name wrong. It couldn't be Burleston after all. It must be some similar sounding place such as Boylestown or Burlesford or even Bakerstown.

"*It is Burleston!*" insisted his brain.

Confusion.

His mind said one thing while his eyes said another. His mind flatly declared, "*This is where you killed Arline.*" His eyes contradicted, "*You don't know this place from Singapore or Seringapatam.*"

Then to make matters worse his mind seemed to split into mutually antagonistic halves. One part gloated, "*Watch out! The police are collecting the evidence. Watch out!*" The other part retorted, "*Damn the police! You've got to prove it to yourself—that's all that matters!*"

Schizophrenia: that was his self-diagnosis. Such a mental condition would account for everything. He was living and had lived for years in two separate worlds. Let not thy right hand know what thy left hand doeth. Let not Bransome the scientist be called to account for Bransome the murderer.

In the last resort it might prove his salvation. They don't execute certified maniacs. They put them away for keeps, in an asylum.

Salvation?

He'd be better off dead!

A heavy-set man lounging in the doorway of a cheap clothing store spoke to him as he strolled past for the sixth or seventh time.

"Looking for someone, stranger?"

Bransome did not hesitate this time. Glib stories come more easily with practice and he'd been getting some of that of late. He had the foresight to make it substantially the same yarn as that fed to the taxi-driver. The gossips in a small town are quick to detect inconsistencies and remark upon them.

"I've been searching for a suggested factory site. Can't find it any place. My informant must have bungled it somehow."

"In Burleston?" asked the other, screwing up his eyes in readiness for deep thought.

"No—just outside the town somewhere."

"What sort of a site? If you can give a description I might be able to help you."

Bransome gave it in as much detail as he could and added, "I'm told that one of the trees has been brought down by a flood." That was a daring item to put in. He waited edgily, half-expecting the other to burst out, "Hey, that's where they found a girl's bones!"

But the other merely grinned and said, "You must be talking of more than half a century ago."

"What d'you mean?"

"I've been here fifty years. We've had no flood any-where around these parts in my time."

"You're sure of that?"

"Couldn't be more positive."

"Perhaps I've got the wrong Burleston."

"I doubt it. I've never heard of another one, not in this part of the world, anyway."

Bransome shrugged, trying to look careless and indifferent. "Nothing for it but to go back and recheck. This trip has been a waste of time and money."

"Tough luck," sympathized the other. "Why don't you try Kaster's real estate office in Hanbury? That fellow knows every farm and field for a hundred miles around."

"It's an idea. Thanks!"

He returned to the bus terminal, baffled. In a town

as small as this an event as large as murder—even an old one recently revived—should be the talk of the place. Proximity to the scene should have made the taxi-driver mention it as the cab went past. The heavy-set man should have responded to the tale of the falling tree with all the lurid details of what the uprooting had revealed. Yet neither had reacted.

It then occurred to him that the local newspaper should be able to provide information without his having to entice it in a manner likely to attract attention. He could have kicked himself for not having thought of it before and he filed the oversight under the heading of criminal amateurism. In spite of days of ducking and dodging he was not yet adept at being on the run.

The current issue of the town paper might contain nothing of significance to him, especially if the case were hanging fire or the police giving no handouts to the press. But some issue in the last few weeks should hold the original story, the theories pertaining to it and perhaps some hint of what was being done about it.

He spoke to a bewhiskered oldster sitting on a nearby bench. "Where's the office of the local paper?"

"We don't have one, mister. We take the *Hanbury Gazette*. It comes out every Friday."

The bus arrived, he got aboard and sat looking through the window. Across the street the beefy man was still loafing in the doorway of his shop, his bored attention on the bus. It was more than certain, Bransome decided, that that observant character would remember him and, if asked, would be able to give a fairly accurate description of him together with times of arrival and departure. He looked like the gabby, miss-nothing type who could come up with damning evidence when required.

Oh, Lord, why were other people's memories so good and his own so bad?

If ever the hunt caught up with him this visit to Burleston might be awkard to explain. He may have made a serious mistake in coming here. Perhaps he should not have given way to the dictates of an abnormal mind or some insistent part of it. The journey could weigh heavily against him when the official questioning began.

"All right, so you're not guilty. Let's accept that. Let's agree that you don't know what we're talking about. Let's agree that you've never heard of Arline Lafarge. Then why did you take it on the lam? Why did you beat it away from home just about as fast as you could go?"

"I didn't beat it. I wasn't running away from anything. I merely treated myself to a week free from work. I was tensed up and needed a rest."

"Did your doctor tell you that?"

"No—I didn't consult my doctor."

"Why not? If you were all that near to collapse he'd have prescribed something, wouldn't he?"

"I wasn't near to collapse and haven't claimed that I was. Don't put words into my mouth."

"We need no instructions from you. Just give straight answers to straight questions. You've nothing to hide, have you?"

"No."

"Okay then. You say you were exhausted and wanted to take it easy for a while?"

"That's right."

"You diagnosed your own trouble and prescribed your own treatment?"

"Yes, I did. There's no law against it."

"We know all about the law. Now answer this: isn't it a wonderful coincidence that you should need a rest way out in the wilds at the very time that we picked up your tracks? Why couldn't you have rested at home, with your wife and kids?"

"We weren't doing each other any good."

"How d'you mean?"

"My mental condition worried them and that added to my worry. It was a vicious circle that aggravated the situation. The worse I felt the worse they made me feel. Seemed to me the only solution lay in taking a few days away from home, somewhere quiet and peaceful."

"Such as Burleston?"

"If I were going away I had to go somewhere, didn't I? I could have gone anywhere, anywhere at all."

"You said it, mister! You could have gone anywhere

59

in the wide, wide world. But you had to go to Burleston. How d'you account for that?"

"I can't account for it."

Perhaps at that point he'd start shouting and they'd give each other sly glances, knowing from experience that he who shouts is in a corner and soon to crack. He'd shout his answers in effort to emphasize his innocence and thereby convince them of his guilt.

"I don't know why I went where I did. I was heading for a nervous breakdown and in no condition for logical thought. I went off at random, believing that the trip would do me good. It was by sheer chance that I ended up in Burleston."

"That and no more?"

"Yes."

"It was just by accident you got to Burleston?"

"Correct."

"You're quite sure about that?"

"I am."

A wolfish grin followed by, "When you left home you told your wife you were going to Burleston. How about that?"

"Did I tell her?"

(Fighting for time, frantic with thought.)

"She says you did."

"She's mistaken."

"Your two kids heard you tell her."

Silence.

"They're mistaken too, eh?"

Silence.

"All three make identically the same mistake, eh?"

"Perhaps I did tell her—though I've no recollection of doing so. I must have had Burleston sort of stuck in my mind and went there without thinking."

"All right. So you went to a God-forgotten dump like that, huh? Most folk around here have never heard of the place. But *you* knew of it. You've just said yourself that it must have been somewhere in your mind. How did it come to be in your mind? What put it there?"

"I don't know."

"Your records show you weren't born in Burleston. You have never lived there. You didn't get married there. Your wife doesn't come from there. On the face of it you have no personal connection with the place. So why did you go there?"

"I've told you a dozen times I don't really know."

"Why did you consider it necessary to tell a bunch of lies about this trip?"

"I didn't. I told my wife where I was going and that is your own evidence."

"Never mind our evidence—you concentrate on yours, such as it is. You told Markham that you were having difficulty with relatives but your wife doesn't know a thing about it. You told your wife you were being sent to Burleston on official business but your superiors flatly deny it. You told a taxi-driver and a shopkeeper that you were looking for a factory site when in fact you were doing nothing of the kind. Isn't that a bunch of lies?"

"I didn't want Markham to know I was feeling lousy."

"Why not?"

"I didn't want him to think I couldn't stand the pace. It doesn't help to give an impression of weakness."

"Doesn't it? Well, all your explanations are weak enough to fall apart. It's quite normal for employees to get sick and say so and be given time off. Why do you regard your case as exceptional?"

Silence.

"How about the fairy tale you told your wife? A man doesn't deceive an attractive woman without good motive."

"She was already deeply concerned for me. I didn't want to add to her worry."

"So you went to Burleston and sought a factory site —or said you were seeking one. We've two witnesses to that. Thinking of setting up in business for yourself? What kind of manufacturing did you have in mind? What products did you plan to turn out? Why locate your plant in Burleston where there is no rail service?"

"The witnesses are mistaken."

"Both of them?"

"Yes."

"H'm! They're suffering from delusions in the same

way as your wife and kids, eh? Strange how everybody gets you wrong, isn't it?"

No reply.

"Medical evidence shows that this girl was murdered. Of all traceable suspects you alone had the opportunity and, we believe, the motive. The crime lies dormant for twenty years while you establish yourself as a loving husband, a good father and a solid citizen. You become a perfect picture of suburban respectability."

Silence.

"Then by a most remarkable coincidence you get tired of it all just after the murder comes to light. By still greater coincidence you decide to take a sudden vacation. In where, of all places? In Burleston!"

Silence.

"Don't let's fool around any longer. We've wasted enough time already. Let's get down to basic facts. The news gave you the jitters because you had good reason for jittering. You had to check up. You had to find out whether the police had got a line on anyone and, if so, who. Otherwise you couldn't sleep at night."

Silence.

"Mister, you're sewed up tight enough to satisfy any jury. A confession is your only hope. At least it may save your neck." A pause, a hard stare, a contemptuous wave of the hand. "Take him away. Let him think it over until his lawyer gets here."

Bransome had no difficulty in imagining the whole dreadful dialogue in which he would be assigned the role of the cornered rat. When the end came would it really be like that? His pulse put in a few extra thumps as he thought of it.

FIVE:

THE QUEASY feeling had passed off by the time he reached Hanbury. He had argued himself out of it on the basis that idle anticipation and ultimate realization can be completely different things. The futute lay in the lap of the gods rather than in the depths of his over-active imagination. The worst might never happen; if it did he would meet it when it came.

He found the office of the *Hanbury Gazette* a few hundred yards from his hotel, went in, said to the lean, sallow-faced youth behind the counter, "Do you have any back numbers available?"

"Depends how far back."

"How about the last three months?"

"Yes, we've plenty. One of each?"

The other dug them out, rolled them into a bundle, put string around them and handed them over. Bransome paid, returned to the hotel and took them up to his room. Locking his door, he opened the bundle on the table by the window and started his examination. For most of two hours he searched through the newspapers page by page, column by column, missing nothing.

These sheets covered a period stretching from last week to three months ago. They recorded a fire, a couple of hold-ups and several car thefts in town, a suicide out of town and a spectacular shooting forty miles away. Nothing out of the ordinary appeared to have happened in or near Burleston.

He could think up two possible explanations for this. First, the trucker who had given forth about the body under the tree may have been misled by talk about a very similar crime located elsewhere. He snatched a gleam of hope from the idea that his burden of guilt might be cast off and borne by another.

Alternatively, the trucker's story might be accurate enough but referred to an event far older than he, Bransome, had assumed. The fellow's manner had not suggested it; on the contrary, he had conveyed the impression of telling about something that had happened fairly recently, within the last few days or perhaps during the previous couple of weeks. The trucker certainly had given the listening Bransome the notion that the news had not had time to grow stale.

Yet again his brain suffered a momentary dizziness. Up to now he had taken it for granted that the powers that be had had only little time in which to trace him; but if, in fact, they had had more than three months they might be very near to him, close upon his heels. Perhaps right at this moment they were in his home firing questions at a pale-faced and distraught Dorothy.

"Where did he tell you he was going? To Burleston? Where the heck is that? See if you can get through to the police there, Joe. Tell 'em he's wanted. If it's not a false lead, they may be able to pick him up."

He sat in his room wrestling with his predicament. From first to last he'd had to cope with a constant succession of panics brought on by his own fears. Now he was managing to develop a resistance to them. Right now the wires might be humming as Dorothy's questioners raised the Burleston or Hanbury police. A day or two ago the mere idea of it would have got him on the run again. But not now. He would sit tight until morning and take a chance on the cops.

It was essential that he remain overnight because the *Gazette* office would have closed by this hour. No more back copies could be got until tomorrow. The part of his mind that battled with his emotions and insisted upon dealing with the situation—the same part that had steered him here—maintained that he must not leave Hanbury without finding what he was seeking or satisfying himself beyond all doubt that it was not there to be discovered. At whatever risk the matter must be settled one way or the other.

Tossing the useless newspapers into the wastebasket, he rubbed his chin and decided to shave before dinner. He unlocked his case, opened it, stood staring at it

64

with deep suspicion. The contents were neatly packed, his belongings intact, nothing missing. Ever since childhood he'd been ludicrously fussy about his packing and, like most people of that type, could tell at a glance when something has been disturbed. Things now lay in his case almost but not quite as he usually placed them. He felt fairly sure that during his absence the case had been emptied and repacked.

He could not be absolutely positive about this but, all the same, he considered it a good guess that someone had opened the case and given the contents a swift and expert examination. Somebody looking for what? In the circumstances there could be only one answer, namely, incriminating evidence. A petty thief, he reasoned, would not have bothered to try to conceal his search by tidily repacking and locking the case. More likely he'd have flung the stuff all over the room to express his anger at finding nothing of value. Only an official searcher would take pains to hide his probing.

He examined the locks for signs of picking or forcing but they showed not a scratch and turned easily. Could he be mistaken about this? Had he unwittingly bounced the suitcase around a bit and thus shaken it up since last it was opened? Or were the Hanbury police already swinging into action?

For the next few minutes he sought carefully through the room for a crushed cigarette butt or a splash of tobacco ash or anything else that could be construed as the mark of an intruder. He found nothing. Neither the bed nor the wardrobe showed the slightest sign of having been disturbed. Proof was non-existent and all he had to go upon was a fussy belief that a spare tie had been folded left to right instead of right to left and that a bunch of handkerchiefs had been packed with points to the rear of the case instead of to the front.

Next, he stood by the window, half-concealed at one side, and watched the street below. He was seeking proof that the hotel was under observation. That got him nowhere, either. Passers-by were numerous but no same figure wandered past twice in twenty minutes and nobody appeared to have even a casual interest in the hotel.

Of course, anyone keeping official watch on the place would not necessarily hang around outside. He might be inside the hotel itself, lounging in the lobby and wearing an innocent air of waiting for someone, or behind the counter posing as a relief clerk. Bransome went downstairs to have a look. The only persons visible in the foyer were two elderly ladies gossiping together; he could not picture either of them in hot pursuit of a murderer. At the counter the one clerk on duty was a skinny runt who could have fitted into a leg of a cop's pants. Bransome went up to him.

"Has anyone called for me while I've been out?"

"No, Mr. Bransome."

"Anyone been shown up to my room?"

"No, sir, not that I know of."

"H'm!"

"Something wrong?" asked the clerk, eyeing him.

"Nothing much. Just had a queer feeling that someone has been prowling around my room."

"Is anything missing?" said the clerk, stiffening himself in readiness for trouble.

"No, nothing at all."

The clerk showed vast relief and suggested, "It may have been the maid."

"Possibly."

Bransome glanced down, ill at ease and vaguely dissatisfied. The hotel register lay wide open and practically under his nose. It was turned to face the clerk but he could see the last entry quite clearly. The fact that the writing was upside-down caused only a little delay in appreciating what he saw. He stared at it absently while his mind churned around until eventually his eyes chipped in and told his brain what was there.

Joseph Reardon. Room 13.

"Thanks," he said to the clerk.

He tramped upstairs, sat on the edge of his bed, and tangled and untangled his fingers while he tried to estimate how many Reardons there might be in the world. Maybe six or seven thousand, maybe ten or more. No knowing, no way of telling. And besides, that lanky, beady-eyed snooper at the plant wasn't necessarily a

Joseph. He could be a Dudley or a Mortimer or anything but a Joseph.

All the same, it was an unpleasant coincidence. Like meeting Reardon at the railroad station was a coincidence. Or having his case tampered with here, right here, just after a Reardon had arrived.

For a short time he seriously considered paying his bill and getting out, not out of town but to some other nearby place where he could stay the night with more assurance of being unwatched. That wouldn't be so easy. It was rather late in the evening, Hanbury had only two hotels, and now would be a poor hour in which to roam the streets seeking a rooming-house.

There was an alternative with which he toyed in the manner of a trapped rat provoked into attacking the cat. He could go to Room 13, boldly knock on the door and confront this Reardon. If the fellow proved to be a complete stranger everything would be all right.

"Sorry, my mistake—wrong room."

But if the occupant of Room 13 turned out to be the one-and-only Reardon there'd be a couple of pointed questions ready for him the moment he opened the door.

"What the hell are you doing here? What's the idea of following me around?"

Yes, it might pay off. Without real proof, Reardon dare not accuse him of anything. If such proof already existed he, Bransome, would now be under arrest. The fact that as yet nobody had seen fit to haul him in gave him an advantage, if only a temporary one.

Filled with sudden resolve he left his room, hurried along the corridor and tapped on the door of Room 13. He was all set to create a scene if the familiar face appeared. He tapped again, more loudly and impatiently. There was no response. Putting an ear to the keyhole he heard not a sound. He knocked longer and still more loudly. Silence. The room was empty. He tried the door-handle and was out of luck; the door remained fastened.

Oncoming feet sounded around the corner of the corridor. Bransome dashed back to his own room, where he left his door a quarter-inch ajar and watched through the crack. A man built on beer-barrel lines tramped past Room 13 and continued steadily onward. Bransome shut and locked his door and gazed meditatively at his suitcase.

In the end he wedged a chair under the door-handle for good measure and got into bed, first having had another long look through the window without finding evidence of a stake-out. For all the good his night's repose did him he could just as well have spent it walking the streets. He missed Dorothy and the kids, pictured them in his mind, wondered when he would see them again. For hours he lay experiencing alternate states of alertness and semi-consciousness, merging himself into a series of fantastic dreams from which the slightest sound brought him fully awake. By dawn he was visibly baggy-eyed and in no mood to sing.

At eight-thirty, the moment it opened, he was at the *Gazette* office. Returning to the hotel, he dumped a large roll of back numbers in his room, then went down to breakfast. A dozen people were sitting around chatting and eating. They included nobody he could recognize. For all that he could tell the whole lot might have been named Reardon, the clerk, the beer-barrel man and the two old ladies to boot.

Breakfast over, he hastened upstairs and sought through the newspapers one by one. They reached back into the past for almost a year. None mentioned his crime. Not one.

For reasons best known to themselves the police might have suppressed the news—but it was incredible that they'd have imposed so complete a blackout for so long. Or was the event more than a year old and reported in an equally older paper? Or had the trucker talked about somebody else's similar misdeed?

He still felt that he had to know one way or the other without tempting fate by his methods of gaining the knowledge. Yet he could think of only one sure and conclusive means of securing the actual facts. It would be a dangerous move *if* he had the courage to make it. It would be tantamount to shoving his head into the lion's mouth. He could go and ask the police about the matter, boldly, frankly, just like that.

Might he get away with it if he gave them a false

name and covered his curiosity with a plausible story? How about describing himself as a professional writer of unsolved mysteries and asking them to help with the data on the case of Arline Lafarge? Jeepers, that might be going too far. He could imagine the cops' reaction.

"Hey, how do *you* know about this? The newspapers have made no mention of it. And how have you got hold of the victim's name? We haven't yet identified her ourselves. Seems to us, mister, that you know a whole lot more than is good for your health. Only one man could know so much—the man who did it!"

Then they'd hold him as a major suspect, eventually discover his true identity, and the fat really would be in the fire. Too risky and too darned stupid. Well, how about calling them from a phone booth? There was an idea. Much as they might like to they couldn't grab a man through a mile of copper wire. Neither could they trace his call and pick him up if he had the sense to refuse to hold on and await their convenience.

He was learning one at a time the tricks and subterfuges of the man on the run. It was a hell of a life.

The booth by the bus station would be the best place. A good tactic would be to consult the time-table there and make his call just before two or three buses were due to depart. If the police came racing to the booth, eager to grab any guilty-looking character in sight, they might be tempted to jump to the wrong conclusions and go haring out of town in pursuit of the buses while he was ruminating his next move back in the comparative safety of the hotel. The police would catch the buses and find themselves stalled for lack of a description of the unknown caller. They'd be unable to pin anything on anyone.

All right, he'd give it a try and with luck persuade authority to let slip something significant over the phone. If, for instance, he asked the police chief whether he needed a line on that case concerning bones found under a tree and the chief showed interest and responded with counter-questions or tried to hold the caller on the line, it would demonstrate the grim reality of the discovery plus the fact that investigators really were working on it.

69

That much decided, he saw no reason for further delay and departed, making sure that both his suitcase and his door were securely locked. He turned and walked swiftly along the carpeted corridor, and came abreast of Room 13 just as its door opened and Reardon started out.

Without a flicker of surprise, Reardon said, "Well, fancy meet—"

He didn't get any further. Bransome slugged him right in the teeth, a vicious blow born of a mixture of fear and fury. Reardon staggered through the still open door and back into his room.

Filled with fierce desperation, Bransome leaped after him and let him have it again, this time smack on the chin. It was a weighty, well-aimed punch that could have knocked out many a man bigger and heavier than the other. But for all his lengthy leanness Reardon was a tough customer. Though taken completely unaware, he refused to go down. He reeled, waved his arms around and tried to regain his balance.

Pressing his advantage to .the full, Bransome gave him no chance to recover. Anger lent him strength such as he had never known. Brushing aside a groggy swing from the other, he planted a haymaker into his gullet. Reardon let out a harsh, choking cough and appeared about to fall. He raised a hand in the air, strove to shout but was unable to give voice.

Bransome landed three more in quick succession before Reardon toppled, not with a clumsy thud but with a quiet folding motion like that of a suddenly emptied suit of clothes. He was a hard egg all right: he could take plenty of punishment. Bransome bent over him, breathing heavily. Glancing behind, he saw that the door was wide open. He went to it and looked along the corridor. Not a soul in sight. Nobody had heard the brief fracas, nobody had raised the alarm. Carefully he closed the door and returned to his opponent.

Standing over Reardon, he rubbed his knuckles as he gazed thoughtfully down. His nerves were taut and his insides still simmering with excitement. This fellow, he decided, was far too smart and persistent a tracker for his comfort. It would be sheer folly not to exploit the

70

present situation and remove the hound-dog from the trail for long enough to make him lose the scent.

Right now he was in a good position to get rid of Reardon once and for all. A man cannot be executed twice for two murders. Yet he couldn't bring himself seriously to consider the idea of killing Reardon there and then. He couldn't have committed so cold-blooded a slaying even for a million dollars. If this had been the right time for useful introspection—which it was not—he'd have perceived the obvious incongruity of a killer balking at a killing and, perhaps, found significance in it.

Despite the fact that the means was ready to hand, he could not have slaughtered Reardon even to gain his own salvation. Reardon lay sprawled partly on his back and partly on one side, his eyes closed, lips bleeding, his jacket open and revealing a small shoulder-holster containing a tiny blued-steel automatic. Bransome eyed the gun speculatively but did not touch it.

Going to the other's luggage-case, Bransome opened it, found therein a dozen handkerchiefs, a couple of ties and all the usual necessities of travel. He used the ties and handkerchiefs to fasten Reardon's wrists and ankles and fix a wad over his crimson mouth. By the time he'd finished Reardon was emitting snuffling noises and showing signs of soon regaining his senses.

Swiftly searching him, Bransome found his wallet and looked through it. Paper money, two or three letters of no special interest, a couple of receipted bills, a folded insurance certificate for a car. One inner flap held postage stamps. The opposite one contained a long, narrow, cellophane-encased card. Bransome studied the card and found his back hairs rising. It bore an embossed eagle, a serial number and some lettering.

Federal Government of the United States
of America.
Department of Military Intelligence.
Joseph Reardon.

71

In the name of all that's holy what had Military Intelligence to do with a plain, sordid murder? It baffled him. The only possible explanation he could think up was that perhaps they took jurisdiction from the police when the homicide involved someone employed on top secret work. But that didn't seem likely. So far as he knew the police administered the law with bland indifference to all other considerations and would march the world's greatest scientist to the death-chamber if justice so ordered.

Anyway, this bloodhound was stalled for the time being. For how much time depended upon how fast he, Bransome, hustled to some place out of reach. Replacing the wallet in the other's pocket, he shoved Reardon behind the bed, sneaked a look out of the door, found nobody in sight. Reardon was now starting to jerk around and emit mumbling noises. Bransome left Room 13, heard the door-latch click behind him.

Dashing to his own room he grabbed his suitcase, had a hasty glance around to make sure nothing was left, went down to the lobby and paid his bill. The clerk was lackadaisical, slow-moving, as if spitefully determined to try Bransome's patience to the limit. While he was detained at the counter Bransome's eyes could not stop looking warily around, seeking a prospective tracker in the lobby, half-expecting an angry rush down the stairs. Snatching his receipted bill, he hurried to the bus station and found no bus due to leave within the next fifty minutes. He then tried the railroad station. No train for an hour and a half.

This meant unwanted and dangerous delay. The instinct of the hunted warned him not to remain in Hanbury a minute longer than could be helped. Temporarily he had abandoned the idea of phoning the police. One could call them from anywhere, even from a thousand miles away. Indeed, when making such a call, distance would lend considerable enchantment to the view.

The main thing was to get out before Reardon broke loose and the powers-that-be sealed the town. He decided to walk along the route of the first bus due to depart; it would pick him up four or five miles out and that might be sufficient to evade the search if in the next fifty minutes Reardon managed to raise the hue and cry. The first things the authorities would do would be to cover the bus and railroad stations, chase all the taxis and question the car-rental offices.

So he trudged out of town, maintaining a good, fast pace and thinking only that he would phone Dorothy before this day was through and find out how she and the children were getting along. Also he'd ask whether anyone had pestered her as to his whereabouts. Once more he was unconsciously displaying his lack of criminal expertness: it had not crossed his mind to steal a car, make a quick getaway, ditch the machine in some big town and confuse the issue by stealing another. He had stolen only once in his life, at age six, the loot being a large apple that had given him the father of all bellyaches.

On the other hand, this touch of the raw novice could have given him a slight advantage had the chase taken the shape he expected of it. From the police viewpoint hardened criminals are predictable within limits; they react thus and so, according to their shadowland logic. The beginner is unpredictable. The old pro just naturally thinks of swift escape in terms of a hot car. The first-timer might do anything, anything at all, even make himself conspicuous by walking on his own two feet. So Bransome walked.

He was lucky at the outset. When he had been twenty minutes on his way, a badly dented and wheezy sedan overtook him, stopped and offered a ride. He accepted, sat himself next to a red-faced, bald, garrulous man and told him truthfully that he'd been ambling along while waiting for the bus to catch up.

"Where ya making for?" asked Redface.

"Any big town." Bransome tapped his case to draw attention to it. "I go from door to door."

"Whatcha selling?"

"Insurance."

Would there never be an end to situations and questions calling for spur-of-the-moment lies?

"What a racket!" declared Redface with complete lack of tact. "My wife nearly got talked into buying a heavy one on me. Like hell you will, I told her. Whyja want me worth more to you dead than alive? Lousy

73

racket, I say. Gives a woman a vested interest in a corpse. That ain't right. There's trouble enough in this world without inviting someone to hit the jackpot by getting a feller into his box."

"Mine's fire and robbery insurance," offered Bransome, soothingly.

"Well, that's a lot different, mister. There's some sense in it. Now my uncle over in Decatur, he had a haybarn go up like a volcano. And him being too stingy even to give at the knees, he lost plenty. I've always said—"

He rambled on and on while the sedan creaked and thumped and burped and knocked off the miles. He listed and described in full detail every major fire for forty years back, and ended by opining that fire-cover was a good bet but the robbery part of it wasn't any bargain because in this part of the country there were few prowlers.

"Easier pickings elsewhere, I guess," he said. "Even a crook won't go a long way just to make it harder for himself."

"Must be nice to have little need of bolts and bars," Bransome commented. "How about murders? Get any of those?"

"Had a few in my time. All of them brought on by booze or women. Only one never got solved."

"Which one was that?" asked Bransome, hoping at long last to hear something worth hearing.

"It was eight or maybe ten years ago," answered Redface, casually. "Old Jeff Watkins got beaten up something awful and died without speaking. The police went looking for a transient who'd been doing odd jobs round and about. They never found him."

"How about that girl they discovered buried under a tree?"

Redface removed his attention from the road long enough to throw him a surprised stare. "Which girl?"

"Maybe it's only a rumor," said Bransome. "A few days ago I overheard someone talking about the bones of a girl being found under a tree outside of Burleston."

"When was this supposed to have happened?"

"I don't know. At least a week ago. Perhaps a few

74

months ago. The fellow didn't seem to be talking about something very old."

"He was talking out of the back of his neck," said Redface, positively.

"Could be."

"If there was anything to it, that story would run like a grass fire for a hundred miles around," asserted Redface. "In these parts they've got to have something to talk about and they talk plenty. I'd be sure to have heard about it."

"But you haven't?"

"No, mister. You must have misunderstood what that fellow was saying." The car rolled into a country town smaller than Hanbury but bigger than Burleston. Redface gave his passenger an inquiring look. "How about here?"

"Suits me—if you're going no farther."

"I can take you another forty miles. After that you'll have twelve more to go to reach the city."

"I'd like that better. I'll take a chance on getting another ride."

"Want to go a good long way, don't you? Think you can't drum up much business in this town?"

"To tell the truth, I'm a bit tired of small places. I think I'd do better in a big one."

"Can't say I blame you," commented Redface. "Doesn't your outfit fix you up with a car?"

"Yes—I left it at home with the wife."

"She got insurance on you?"

"Yes, of course."

"Women," said Redface, scowling ahead. "Bunch of grab-alls. Take everything a man's got."

He fell silent, gnawing steadily at his bottom lip as the car trundled straight through the town and out the other side. The increasing mileage suited Bransome, who felt that the more of it the better. The driver continued to hold his peace, apparently irritated by the iniquities of the female sex.

They came to a point about thirty miles from the last town and ten from Redface's destination. Here they joined a wide, straight artery on which two cars were stalled. The sedan rattled nearer and nearer. A uniformed figure broke away from the group by the two cars and stood in the middle of the road. It was a state trooper holding up a forbidding hand.

One of the halted cars started up and purred away just as Redface said, "What now?" and braked to a stop. A second trooper appeared beside the first. The pair cautiously approached the sedan, one on either side. Their manner showed them to be more interested in the passengers than the car.

Looking inside, the taller of the two said to Redface, "Why, hello Wilmer! How's tricks?"

"So-so," growled Redface, not overjoyed. "Whatcha want to bitch about this time?"

"Take it easy, Wilmer," advised the other. "We're looking for someone." He gestured toward Bransome. "Know this fellow?"

"Should I?"

"He's riding with you, isn't he?"

"Sure is. You want to make something of it?"

"Now look, Wilmer, let's be sensible about this, shall we? I'm not married to you and I don't have to take any of your lip. So let's have a few straight answers. Where'd you find this character?"

"Picked him up outside Hanbury," Redface admitted.

"You did, did you?" The trooper studied Bransome with care. So did his partner. "You correspond more or less with the description of our man."

"That grieves me," said Bransome.

"What's your name?"

"Carter."

"And what d'you do for a living?"

"I'm an insurance salesman."

"That's right," confirmed Redface, maliciously glad to give some support. "We've been talking about it. I told him about the time that gabby greaseball tried to get Maisie to make a wad outa my body and—"

"Carter, eh?" said the first trooper, taking no notice of Redface. "What's your first name?"

"Lucius," informed Bransome, digging it up from God only knew where and handing it out fast.

This promptness made the questioners a mite uncertain. They glanced at each other and examined Bransome again, obviously making mental comparisons with a description given over the radio.

"What were you doing in Hanbury?" asked one.

"Selling insurance." Bransome put on a wry smile. "Or trying to."

He flattered himself that he was getting pretty good at this falsehood business. All one needed was plenty of practice and excellent control of the nerves. Nevertheless, he inwardly regretted his newfound aptitude. By nature he detested lies and liars.

"Got any proof of your identity?" asked the shorter trooper.

"I don't think so. Not with me, I leave most of my personal documents at home."

"Nothing in your case or wallet? No letters, cards or anything like that?"

"Sorry, I haven't."

"Strange for an insurance salesman to roam around without a single thing to show who he really is, isn't it?" The shorter trooper thinned his lips, threw his partner a warning look. "I think you'd better get out of this dilapidated hearse, Mr. Lucius Carter." Jerking open the door, he gestured authoritatively. "We'd like a closer look at you and what you've got."

Bransome dismounted with something in his mind saying, *"This is it! This is it!"* Back of him Redface sat behind the wheel and looked embittered. The shorter trooper reached into the car, pulled out the suitcase and dumped it on the road. The other trooper posed warily a few yards away, hand on gun-butt. No use running for it. The trooper standing at the ready could put a slug in his back before he'd covered ten yards.

"Your wallet and keys, please."

Bransome handed them over.

The other looked carefully through the evidence, grunted with satisfaction, said to his partner, "Lucius Carter in a pig's eye! This is the fellow, Richard Bransome." He gave Redface a wave of dismissal. On your way, Happy."

Redface reached out an arm, violently slammed the

77

open door and yelled through the window, "Dilapidated hearse my foot! I bought this heap myself, with my own money. And as a taxpayer I bought yours as——"

The taller trooper put his face close to Redface's and said very quietly and slowly, "You're a big boy now, Wilmer. You heard what the nice man said. *Get going!*"

Wilmer savagely revved up, favored Bransome and the troopers with a defiant glare, jerked the car forward with a bang and a cloud of oily gas.

"Get in, mister," said the shorter trooper to Bransome. He signed to the patrol car.

"Why should I? What am I supposed to have done? If you've anything against me, say so."

"You'll hear all about it at headquarters," snapped the trooper. "We can hold you for twenty-four hours on suspicion of anything. So quit the back-chat and get in."

Dropping further argument, Bransome entered the patrol car. Shorty piled into the back and sprawled beside him. The other trooper took the driver's seat, flipped a switch and spoke into a hand-microphone.

"Car Nine, Healy and Gregg. We've just picked up Bransome and are bringing him in."

SIX:

At headquarters their attitude toward him was peculiar to say the least. They treated him offhandedly but without any of the toughness usually shown to a major suspect. It seemed as though they were far from sure of his real status, did not know if he had blown up the U.S. Treasury or was a missing candidate for the Congressional Medal. After making further check on his identity, they gave him a meal, put him in a cell and asked no questions.

All he got in reply to his own queries was the curt order, "Shut up and wait."

Reardon arrived three hours later. A couple of blobs of medicated plastic sealed the splits in his lips, otherwise he showed no visible damage. They gave him a small office where he sat and waited patiently until they brought Bransome in.

Left alone, the two faced each other blank-faced and without emotion and Reardon said, "I guess you know you've laid yourself wide open to a charge of common assault?"

"Go ahead with it then," answered Bransome, shrugging.

"Why did you do it? Why did you go for me like that?"

"To teach you to mind your own damn business."

"I see. You objected to me being around?"

"Of course. Who wouldn't?"

"Most people wouldn't," Reardon declared. "Why should they? They've nothing to conceal. What are *you* trying to hide?"

"Find out."

"I'm trying to do that right now. Care to tell me?"

Bransome gazed blankly at the wall. So far the subject of murder had not been broached. That was strange, seeing that they had come after him and taken him in. Perhaps Reardon was saving it for the last, smacking his broken lips over the accusation yet to come. A sadist enjoying a cat-and-mouse act.

"I may be able to help you," continued Reardon, still calm and collected. "I *want* to help you."

"How nice," said Bransome.

"But it's impossible to help without knowing what you've got in your hair."

"Lice," Bransome informed.

Reardon said sharply, "This isn't a cheap vaudeville act. It's a serious business. If you're in a jam of some kind and need assistance, you'll have to talk."

"I can look after myself."

"Running away from your job, home and family is a mighty poor way of doing it."

"I'm the judge of that."

Reardon growled, "So am I. Fix it firmly in your mind that I'm going to get to the bottom of this in any way I can."

"The bottom of what?" asked Bransome, sardonically. "I've taken a short vacation, properly applied for and officially permitted. That was legal enough at the time I left the plant. I'm not aware that they've changed the law since."

Giving a deep sigh, Reardon said, "I can see you don't intend to open up—just yet. That leaves me no option but to take you back. We'll discuss the matter further on the way home."

"You can't take me back," Bransome contradicted. "Common assault isn't an extraditable offense."

"That charge hasn't and won't be entered," Reardon gave back. "It'll be a sad day when I run to the law because of a slap in the face. You'll come back with me of your own free will—"

"Or what?"

"Or I'll plaster you with a federal charge of suspected disloyalty and dissemination of official secrets. After that you'll go exactly where you're told, at the double, and like it."

Bransome felt himself going crimson as he rasped, "I am not a traitor."

80

"Nobody has suggested that you are."

"You've just done so yourself."

"I've done nothing of the sort," Reardon denied. "Up to the present I've found no reason to think your loyalty other than watertight. But when it's necessary I'm willing to fight fire with fire. So I've told you of the dirty trick I won't hesitate to employ to get you back at all costs and uncover whatever it is that you're hiding."

"That means you're prepared to smear me with a false accusation?"

"Correct. I shall have no scruples whatsoever."

"And you want to help me?"

"I certainly do."

"Well," said Bransome, "that gives me two theories —either you're crazy or you think that I am."

"For all I know you may be off your head," responded Reardon. "If so, I want to know how you got that way all of a sudden."

"Why?"

"Because you aren't the first and in all probability you won't be the last."

Bransome narrowed his eyes at him and said, "What the devil are you talking about?"

"I'm talking about loonies. I'm talking about sane and intelligent men who suddenly become irrational. We've been getting too many of them. It's time it was stopped."

"I don't understand and furthermore I don't want to. All I can say is that if you're convinced that a man is crazy to take a vacation and get a much-needed rest, well, you must be a bit touched in the head yourself."

"You weren't taking a vacation."

"Wasn't I?"

"If you were you'd have had the wife and kids along."

"You seem to know my motives better than I do myself," remarked Bransome, dryly. "What do you think I have been doing?"

"Running away from something. Or, alternatively, running after something. More likely the former."

"Running away from what?"

"*You* tell *me*," suggested Reardon, eyeing him pointedly.

"It's your theory and not mine. You produce some data in support of it. Put up or shut up."

Frowning to himself, Reardon consulted his watch. "I can't stay here all day arguing to no useful purpose. There's a train due to leave in twenty minutes' time. We'll just about make it if we go now." He paused, added, "Are you coming of your own accord or do you prefer to be dragged?"

"I'd rather be dragged. I might then be able to soak you for heavy damages."

"You've some hopes. Any competent lawyer will tell you that suing the government gets you nowhere. Besides, I know what I'm doing. I can sustain a plea of justification."

"All right, let's get that train."

Bransome stood up, feeling yet again that it was mentally impossible to sort things out. Not a word had been said about Arline Lafarge. The threat hanging over him was a direct threat to his life or at least his liberty. But for some mysterious and incomprehensible reason they were substituting a different and vaguely defined menace.

When deliberately and with premeditation a man kills a woman, it is murder, morally and legally murder. That's a plain, inescapable fact that the law has to cope with a dozen or more times a month. Yet here was an instance where the civil law seemed impotent and the military power was intervening to pronounce him not guilty by reason of insanity.

Why?

It beat him utterly.

As the train snaked through the countryside, Reardon started on him again. "Now see here, Bransome, I'm going to be frank with you. For heaven's sake be on the level with me. I'm going to tell you why I've a special interest in you. In return, I want you to tell what you're hiding, what has got you on the run."

"I'm not on the run."

"Not now, perhaps. Not since I caught up with you. But originally you were."

"I was not. It's merely your delusion."

"Let's. quit banging our skulls together; we'll get nothing out of it other than a pain in the nut. I want to remind you of something you seem to have forgotten, namely, the fact that there's a war on. It's not a shooting war but it's a war just the same. Why else should you and many others be working full time on the development of newer and better weapons?"

"Well?"

"Weapon-work goes on in case the cold war becomes hot. In the interim a non-shooting war is fought by non-shooting methods. Each side tries to steal the other's best brains, or buy them over, or sabotage them or destroy them outright. We have lost men and ideas and plans. So have they. We've bought over some of their brains. They've acquired some of ours. See what I mean?"

"Of course. It's old stuff."

"Old or not, it still operates." Reardon's lean face and sharp eyes looked snoopier than ever. "The weapons in a non-shooting war are those of theft, bribery, blackmail, seduction, murder, anything and everything that is effective for its purpose. They can and do cause casualties on both sides. The logical method of fighting a non-shooting war is to employ every available means of increasing the enemy's losses while, at the same time, preventing or reducing one's own. The latter is fully as important as the former—and the latter is my job. It's the responsibility of my department to beat off attacks on our brainpower."

"You're telling me nothing that's new and wonderful," Bransome complained. "And so far as I'm concerned it's a hell of a thing when a fellow can't take time off without being suspected of planning to sell what he's got in his head."

"You're oversimplifying the situation," Reardon asserted. "Basically there are two ways of weakening the enemy. You can acquire his brains for your own use or, if that proves impossible, you can deprive him of the use of them. It's a dog-in-the-manger policy: if I can't employ that genius, neither can you, see? So let's say that inherently you're too loyal to sell what you've got in your head. What then?"

"So what then?"

"The enemy removes your head so that if he can't have it neither can anyone else."

"Bunk! I'm not worth the bother of decapitating."

"That's like saying a soldier isn't worth the bother of sending to the battlefront. As one single, solitary individual, maybe he isn't. But as a hundred, a thousand or ten thousand individuals he becomes a formidable force that can make all the difference between defeat and victory." Reardon stopped for a moment to let his words sink in, then said, "Personally I could not care less about one Bransome. I'm worried about a hundred or a thousand Bransomes."

"You've got one consolation," Bransome pointed out. "*My* head is still tight on my shoulders."

"I've been speaking metaphorically, as you're well aware. A brain that suddenly refuses to continue working for its country is a valuable intelligence lost to that country. It's a casualty in the undeclared war. In this highly technological age the deadliest strike one can make against a foe is to deprive him of his brains, whether or not one acquires them oneself. Either way it's a setback."

"That's obvious," agreed Bransome. "Any fool can see it and—without boasting—I did my sums many years ago. But I still don't see how all this applies to me right now."

"I'm getting to that," Reardon responded. "Some good men have been lost within the last couple of years, not only from your plant but also from several others. They are over and above the quota of natural losses attributable to retirement, illness or death. If we don't devise some way of stopping it the company will become a regiment and the regiment will become an army." He made a sweeping gesture. "After that—*blooey!*"

"Are you sure the losses aren't natural?" asked Bransome, remembering the suspicions he had voiced to Berg.

"We're pretty sure. We're next door to positive. What is bad is that it took us far too long to realize that something extraordinary was happening. All the casualties were trustworthy and valuable men. All

84

started falling down on their jobs, acting out of character and generally going to pieces. Some deteriorated quicker than others. Some took off without so much as a sweet goodbye. Others resigned or sought leave of absence or took a vacation from which they didn't return. Several of them faded across the border. We know what they are doing today and it's nothing contrary to this country's interest. But we can't bring them back without extraditable reason. So long as they behave themselves in the country of their choice they can stay put for keeps and there's nothing we can do about it. Recently we traced and caught up with three still in this country."

"And what happened?"

"All three stood pat on their fundamental right to live where they like and do any kind of work they please. Their jobs weren't as good as the ones they'd thrown up but they insisted that they preferred them and were under no obligation to explain the preference. In the opinion of the agents who reported on them, all three were scared about something or other. It was obvious that they resented being traced and questioned."

"Can't say I blame them," Bransome offered. "I detest being tracked like a felon. I didn't smack you in the teeth for nothing. I felt it was high time you learned to live and let live."

Taking no notice, Reardon continued, "Soon afterward they disappeared again, were retraced to other places and other jobs. We decided to keep an eye on them without bothering them any further. We were compelled to face the ugly fact that brains had ceased to work for this country and we had no way of compelling them to do so. There lies the weakness of our virtues; some other kind of regime could and would exercise compulsion."

"So you've got me tagged as the next rebel on the list?" asked Bransome, immensely relieved at finding that the real reason for his antics remained unknown and unsuspected.

"You and another," Reardon informed. "The day we decided to smell along your footprints we took off after a fellow elsewhere. He'd been showing the same symptoms."

"Caught up with him yet?"

"No—but we will eventually." Reardon went on with, "Unknown to you, we had sent a flier around all weapon-research establishments asking for prompt information on any employees who left their jobs suddenly or showed signs of cracking or who were behaving strangely in any way. That's how we got a line on you."

"Who put you on to me?"

"Not telling," said Reardon, flatly. "It was someone who considered that you were no longer your sweet little self."

"Cain for a bet," hazarded Bransome. "He's always fancied himself as an amateur psychologist."

"I'm not playing guessing games, so don't think you can identify the culprit by process of elimination."

"All right—I'll accept that some yap yapped."

"So I came along. I looked over the evidence, followed you around, decided that definitely you had the fidgets and might be about to throw things over. It takes something, really something, to persuade a man to rid himself of good pay, good prospects and security. We want to know what does it. If we can discover that much, we can put a stop to it."

"In my case you're going to have a hard time preventing something that has never been started," Bransome advised.

"I don't believe you. Know what I think? I think you are reacting to some serious threat to yourself or to your wife and children."

Bransome said nothing.

"There's no threat that can't be met and countered," argued Reardon, encouraged by the other's silence. "We can meet it and beat it provided we know exactly what it is. Otherwise we're left to fumble in the dark." His penetrating eyes studied Bransome with care. "If somebody is being menaced, tell us who and how. We'll tend to it, you can bet your life on that!"

Hah, that was a laugh! The government would give protection to a malefactor that it would be obliged to punish if the truth became known. Reardon was talking about an enemy on the other side of the planet, when all the time the real foe was The Law armed with the gas chamber and the electric chair.

The intervention of Military Intelligence was now explained. They and the police were working at cross-purposes without knowing it. The former suspected him of suffering mysterious coercion to dodge his duties. The latter had failed—so far—to pick up a lead that would take them to a killer. It was disconcerting to know that the M.I. had him wrongly classified as a prospective deserter but mightily comforting to learn that the cops remained stalled.

"Am I right?" persisted Reardon. "Is somebody's life being threatened?"

"No."

"You're a liar."

"Have it your own way," said Bransome, wearily.

Half twisting in his seat, Reardon looked through the window and watched the passing scenery while the train thundered on. He remained quiet for several minutes, immersed in his thoughts. Suddenly he turned and spoke.

"Where does this dump Burleston fit into the picture?"

Despite himself Bransome jerked and changed color. The unexpected question came like a kick in the stomach.

"What d'you mean?"

"You're still trying to dodge the issue but your face has given you away. Burleston means something to you, something dark and desperate, yet something you just had to seek."

"If you know so darned much about it you should know what it is."

"I don't know. What's more, I don't think you found it." Reardon kept close watch upon him, trying to analyze his reactions. "I can make a guess as to why your gallivantings were in vain."

"Go right ahead if guessing amuses you," Bransome invited.

"You expected to make contact with somebody unknown to you, on his initiative. But I messed it up. It was seen that you were being followed and somebody didn't like my face. Therefore he didn't get into touch with you as arranged. Or perhaps he didn't give you whatever he'd promised to give."

"He? Who's 'he'?"

"A representative of the opposition. So don't pretend to be innocent—you know quite well who I mean."

"You've a very large bee in your bonnet. You can't hear anything but its buzzing."

"Now look, Bransome, I'm much better informed than you may think. You traipsed around Burleston like a lost soul in Hades, looking for something you could not find or waiting for something that never arrived. Lovely way to spend a vacation, isn't it?"

Bransome offered no comment.

"You bought umpteen back issues of the *Hanbury Gazette,* presumably because you have an insatiable appetite for old news. I take it you sat in your bedroom and conscientiously read them all. Nothing like out-of-date gossip for relieving nervous strain, is there?"

Bransome pulled a face and did not reply.

"You spoke to a number of people in Burleston and Hanbury. Last night we checked on all of them, looking for evidence of foreign connections. It got us nowhere —they were as clean as new-born pups. You or somebody else took alarm from the fact that you were under observation and became too smart to give us a clue to what you were looking for."

"I was searching for a red-haired chiropodist. There aren't many in the world."

"I know, I know," said Reardon, huffily.

"Now I'll tell you something," Bransome went on, "and it's this: the hardest thing to find is that which doesn't exist."

"Whatever you were seeking does—or did—exist. A man of your mental caliber doesn't grope around for nothing."

"As I said before, bunk!"

"You're as bad as the three I've mentioned. Won't talk. Won't give answers that make sense. Fall back on the defensive by saying there's no law against them doing whatever they're supposed to be doing."

88

"What they're doing may be innocent enough," said Bransome.

"Which is more than can be said for what you've been up to," Reardon snapped back. "Henderson, at least, did turn to operating a hardware store. And he did offer his reasons, such as they were: 'I like it, I prefer working for myself, I get a lot of satisfaction out of it, I'm not subjected to continual regimentation, I enjoy being independent.' "

"Pretty good reasons, if you ask me."

"I am not asking you. The reasons were not the whole truth and we know it—but we don't know what the whole truth is. We first found Henderson in Calumet. He was questioned. A month later he sold his business and cleared out. A couple of weeks ago we managed to trace him again. We got a lead to another small hardware business at Lakeside and sure enough he was running that one. So we're keeping an eye on him from a discreet distance. He has an ulterior motive for avoiding official attention. So have you!"

Bransome simulated complete boredom and silently gazed through the window.

"You were in a jam and had to go to Burleston to find a way out. I don't know what shape or form that escape was supposed to take but it's my bet that you didn't find it. So where does that put you? It puts you right back where you started. You're still in a jam. You scooted from home and ran around Burleston like a trapped rat and it hasn't done you one bit of good."

"Oh, shut up!" Bransome growled.

"The devil on your back did not obligingly dismount in Burleston as you'd hoped he would. He hung on tight and he's still riding you. He'll go on riding until you come to your senses and let someone else pull him off, someone better able to get at him. For a start, all you need do is open your mouth and name him."

"Pardon me." Bransome stood up and offered a weary smile. "I want to see a dog about a man."

With that he got up from the seat before the surprised Reardon could decide what to do about it. A pretext for stopping him or insisting on accompanying him was not easy to think up in a split second. After all, he was not under arrest and had not been charged with a crime. As of that moment he was free, adult and ordinary, with the status of a normal passenger on a normal train.

Out of one eye as he turned to hasten along the corridor he saw Reardon come to his feet, slowed by indecision. Speeding up, he went to the toilet, fastened its door, opened its window and had a quick look out. Then he clambered through the window. For a couple of seconds he stood with his feet on the window-ledge, his fingertips hooked in the guttering of the coach roof, his body buffeted by the train's slipstream. He flung himself away.

SEVEN:

HE HIT a heavily grassed bank sloping steeply downward. Although he managed to land on his feet his forward momentum and the sharp angle of the bank sent him tumbling diagonally down the slope in a series of violent rolls during which he did his best to keep himself curled into a ball. The world rotated around him and thumped him all over. The bank seemed to be a mile high and he thought he was never going to reach the bottom of it. Eventually he landed with a crash in a dry ditch, breathless and dirty, his nostrils choked with dust.

For a short time he lay there gasping for air, sneezing repeatedly and listening to the dying vibrations along the overhead track. The train showed no sign of stopping; steadily it pounded onward bearing a thwarted Reardon who was losing distance with every second that it took him to swing into action. Reardon might well be carried twenty miles or more before he could make sure of Bransome's getaway and do something about it.

Or had the sharp-eyed agent anticipated the leap for liberty and taken a dive himself? Bransome came erect in the ditch, straightening himself slowly and apprehensively lest he suddenly feel the agony of a broken bone. He felt himself all over, finding no damage other then to his clothes. The escape could not have been better performed had he been doing it for the movies.

That last thought came back a second time as if to lend itself emphasis: it couldn't have been better performed had he been doing it for the movies. His mind gave another jolt, one hard enough to make him pause as he was about to scramble from the ditch. The movies? *The movies?*

Strange that a random idea about motion pictures should hit him like that. Once upon a time he'd considered the movies in an absent kind of way much as one thinks of dogs or doughnuts, hats or hamburgers or any other commonplace appurtenances of civilization. But now it was different without any obvious reason for the difference. Now he though of movies with a peculiar sense of strain that wasn't exactly fear or terror; it was something else, something he couldn't quite identify. The nearest he could get to defining his mental attitude was to say that the concept of motion pictures was accompanied by a sense of basic incongruity or of something that violated a fundamental law in a way that hurt him personally.

Perhaps Reardon had been right in suggesting that he was off his head or rapidly going that way. Perhaps as his mental condition became worse he would experience weird thoughts and have cockeyed reactions every hour instead of a few times a week. Then in the end he would live in a hell of illusions beyond the bars of which a tearful Dorothy would be seen only in rational moments.

Climbing from the ditch, he scrambled up the bank and looked along the railroad track. The train had gone from sight and no scratched and dust-covered Reardon was visible to provide unwelcome company. Satisfied with that, he took another inward look at himself and decided that no matter what might be wrong with him it wasn't insanity. When he made the effort to control his emotions he could study himself objectively and decide that he was not crazy, he was merely a man with an abnormal load of worry on his mind and he had to get rid of it by any means he could devise.

Walking back along the track he came eventually to a bridge over a dirt road. He left the track, went down the bank and onto the road. Which direction would be best to take was a matter of guesswork and he had no time to sit around and wait for information from a rare passer-by. It was a sure bet that before long Reardon's inquisitive gaze would be going over a large-scale map while he figured out the points at which the fugitive might be intercepted.

So he turned to the left and half-walked, half-ran for two miles along the narrow, rutted way. Here he joined a better surfaced secondary road, turned left again and ten minutes later was picked up by a farm truck overloaded with vegetables. Showing no interest whatever in his passenger's identity or purposes, the laconic driver took him twenty miles to town and dropped him with a curt nod.

This place, the nearest to his escape-point, was or soon would be a dangerous area in which he'd be foolish to linger. He caught the next bus out, thanking the gods because—having abandoned his suitcase on the train—he still retained his wallet and his money.

The bus covered sixty miles before reaching a fairly large town. Conscious of his scruffy appearance, Bransome stopped there long enough to wash, shave and brush up. It did much to help his confidence. He followed it with a meal that restored his energy. From the restaurant he returned to the bus terminal, passing two cops on the way. Both policemen were idling on corners, and neither took undue note of him or registered so much as mild curiosity. Evidently the alarm had not yet reached this far, though it might come at any time.

An express bus was soon to leave for a city seventy-five miles to the east. He took it and arrived without incident and became an elusive unit in the crowds. Nothing helps anonymity more than to become lost in a very large herd.

In this city he was quite a jump nearer home. Home! He found himself longing to hear and talk to the voice that personified home. For all he knew his domestic phone might be tapped, its incoming calls monitored and suspicious ones traced. A call to Dorothy might give official listeners a rough idea of his present whereabouts. But it was a risk he wanted to take for the sake of the lift it would give to his morale. Besides, this city would be difficult to search, far more so than small places like Burleston and Hanbury. If he used his wits he could live here for a month with every cop in the place looking for him.

93

A bank of phone booths stood in the hall of the central post office. Choosing the middle one, he put his call through. Dorothy answered at once.

He did his best to make his voice sound cheerful and heartening as he greeted, "Hi, sweet! This is your absent lover."

"Rich!" she exclaimed. "I was expecting to hear from you last night."

"You had a narrow escape. I intended to call but couldn't make it. A gabby character monopolized my time. So I decided to phone today. Better late than never, eh?"

"Yes, of course. How are you making out? Are you feeling better?"

"Topnotch," he lied. "What goes there?"

"We're okay. Everything is as usual—except that there've been a couple of odd incidents."

"What happened?"

"The day after you left somebody phoned, allegedly from the plant, and wanted to know where you'd gone."

"What did you say?"

"The query seemed strange to me seeing that you'd gone on official instructions. So I told this caller to ask in the appropriate department."

"How did he like that?"

"I don't think he did like it," said Dorothy, her tones expressing a touch of anxiety. "He cut off as if annoyed. Oh, Rich, I hope I haven't riled someone important."

"You did quite right," he soothed.

"That's not all," she went on. "A couple of hours later two men called here. They said they were from the plant's security Section and showed me a document to prove it. One was a tall, lean, beady-eyed type, the other a close-cropped and slightly over-muscled character. They told me I had no cause for alarm and that they were doing some routine cross-checking. Then they asked whether you'd told me where you were going and, if so, what you'd said about it. So I told them you'd gone to Burleston but had not offered any reason. They said that was quite satisfactory and they chatted a short time and left. They were pleasant enough in a deadpan kind of way."

94

"Anything more?"

"Yes. The following morning a big, heavily built man knocked at the door. He asked for you and somehow I felt that he knew quite well that you weren't here. I told him you'd gone away for a short while. He wanted to know where and for how long. He wouldn't give me his name or state his business and I didn't like his evasiveness—so I suggested he go ask his questions at the plant. I got the impression that he didn't care to do that, I can't imagine why. Anyway, I got rid of him."

"Probably it was the fellow who'd phoned the day before," guessed Bransome, mulling it over.

"I don't think it was the same man. His voice sounded quite different."

"What did he look like?"

Being observant, she was able to describe the visitor in some detail. The resulting picture bore a close resemblance to the individual who had stared at him in the snack bar's mirror and had followed him home a couple of times. Offhand, he could not think of anyone else coming closer to Dorothy's description.

"And he wouldn't say why he wanted to see me?"

"No, Rich." She paused, went on, "Perhaps I'm being silly about this but at the time I felt convinced that he didn't really wish to see you at all. He wanted to make sure that you weren't here, that you'd actually gone away. I got the definite impression that he expected me to refuse further information and wasn't surprised or disappointed when I did."

"Could be."

"He was most polite, I'll give him his due for that. He was smooth and courteous in the way that some foreigners are."

"Huh?" Bransome pricked up his ears. "You think he was a foreigner?"

"I'm sure of it. He had the mannerisms. He spoke with complete fluency but had a slightly guttural accent."

"Did you phone the two from the plant and tell them about this?"

"No, Rich, I didn't. Should I have? There didn't seem to be anything worth telling."

"Forget it—it's not important."

He gossiped a bit more, learned how the children were behaving, swapped a little badinage, warned her that his return home might be delayed a few days. Hanging up, he left the booth in a hurry, feeling that his call had taken dangerously long. He walked the streets while stewing over this latest information and wondering what it really meant.

If the last mysterious visitor were in fact the person he suspected him to be, and if Dorothy's instinct ran true in identifying him as a foreigner, his original diagnosis must be wrong. The fellow was not a cop in plain clothes or an official agent of any kind. He was a watcher, no doubt of that, but not one appointed by authority.

So firstly someone had phoned, supposedly from the plant, and got no satisfaction. Then Reardon and a stooge had called in person; therefore, for reasons unknown, the former had not followed him from the station but had gone to Hanbury a day or two later. Possibly Reardon had considered it advisable to report back, discuss the matter with somebody and double-check with Dorothy before taking off in pursuit.

Then there was this final caller, a foreigner. The only logical conclusion was that two separate and distinct groups were mutually interested in his movements.

Neither of them were police.

Yet the police were the only ones with a right to be interested and with a motive for nailing him down. The more he thought it over the crazier it seemed. There must be method in all this madness. A solution lay somewhere if only it could be found.

Bransome spent the night in a small rooming-house in the suburbs. It was a sleazy dump a few grades better than a rat-hole but its owner, a sour-faced, angular female, looked fully capable of keeping her trap shut and minding her own business. This virtue, Bransome suspected, brought her a steady clientele of people who had reasons for wanting above-average privacy. He had found the place by asking the advice of the corner newsboy, a wizened and toothless character who evidently regarded a straw mattress as a status symbol.

By ten o'clock Bransome was back in the center of the city. He sought and found the public library, applied for an almanac and settled down to consult it in the reading room. It turned out that there were numerous Lake Thisses and Lake Thattas, several Laketowns, Lakevilles, Lakehursts, Lakeviews, and no less than four Lakesides. Only the latter interested him. He dug out more details about them. One had a population of four hundred, another a mere thirty-two. Although he knew nothing about the hardware trade he considered it an intelligent guess that neither of these two was large enough to support a business of that type. The other Lakesides looked more promising, each having approximately two thousand citizens. Which of the pair should he try?

After some thought he decided that there was no way of identifying the right one here and now, not even by phone calls. He'd have to take a chance and go and look at them. From the expenditure point of view it was sensible to choose the nearer of the two for first inspection. It would be a waste of valuable time and hard-earned cash to travel farther than he had to.

He made his way to the main-line station, keeping watch around him on the approach road, at the ticket office and on the departure platform. All stations, bus or train, were focal points of cross-country movement and therefore, he theorized, the favorite haunts of watchers and seekers. They were like water-holes in arid country: they functioned as common meeting-places for the hunters and the hunted. So he remained on the alert until his train arrived. By the time he climbed aboard he had discovered nobody paying him extra-special attention.

The journey took a large part of the day. In the early evening he walked into the main street of a small, easy-going town set in heavily wooded country. A long, narrow lake glistened on the southern side. Bransome entered a cafeteria, had coffee and sandwiches, spoke to the attendant.

"Know of a hardware store near here?"

97

"Addy's," responded the other. "One block up and around the corner."

"Has it changed ownership recently?"

"I wouldn't know, George."

"Thanks!" said Bransome, thinking that in a place this size everybody usually knows everything about everybody else.

Leaving, he looked along the street and found it impossible to tell which way was "up" and which "down." Oh, well, it didn't matter; he'd make a guess at it. Turning right, he walked one block, rounded the corner and found he had chosen correctly. He was facing a small store that carried on its signboard the words: *Addy's Hardware*. Pushing open its door, he went inside.

There were two customers in the shop, one buying a coil of fence-wire, the other inspecting an oilstove. The former was being served by a lanky youth with a ducktail haircut. The latter was being attended by a thickset, bespectacled man who glanced up as Bransome entered, gave a brief flash of surprised recognition and continued talking about the oilstove. Bransome sat himself on a keg of nails, and waited until the buyers had been served and taken their departure.

Then he said, "Hi, Henny!"

Far from delighted, Henderson growled, "What do *you* want?"

"That's what I call a hearty welcome," said Bransome. "Aren't you pleased to see an old colleague?"

"I was under the impression that I knew you only by sight and name. If we're close pals it's news to me."

"Sight and name are plenty good enough to start an everlasting friendship, aren't they?"

"You didn't come all this way just to kiss me," Henderson gave back nastily. "So get down to brass tacks. What d'you want?"

"A talk with you—in private."

"Who sent you here?"

"Nobody. Not a soul. I've come entirely on my own initiative."

"A likely story," commented Henderson, openly irked. "I presume you found my address in your crystal ball?"

"No, I did not."

"Then how did you get it? Who gave it to you?"

"I can explain in full and to your satisfaction if we can have a discussion somewhere nice and quiet." He held up a stalling hand as Henderson was about to make a retort, and added, "This is no place for chewing the fat or coming to blows. How about my seeing you later, after you've closed the store?"

Henderson frowned and said unwillingly, "All right. Make it eight o'clock. Ring at the side door."

Bransome left as another customer came in. Outside, he recalled Reardon's remark to the effect that a discreet watch was being kept upon Henderson. Such observation would take note of all visitors and, perhaps, succeed in identifying one wanted elsewhere. He looked up, down and across the street in hope of spotting the watcher, but that individual was excessively discreet or possibly off duty. Nobody was keeping an eye on the place so far as he could detect.

How to spend the intervening time was something of a problem; to stroll to and fro along the main street for a couple of hours would be to draw attention to himself and that was the last thing he wished. He solved that difficulty by taking the road to the lake an strolling along its verge like a sightseer enjoying the view. Eventually becoming bored, he returned to town still with half an hour to spare. Another light meal took care of that, using the same cafeteria as before.

"Coffee, black, Albert. And a ham sandwich."

The attendant brought them, unceremoniously dumped them in front of him. Then he leaned across the counter.

"Sixty cents. And the name isn't Albert."

"How right you are." Bransome gave him the money, said, "And the name isn't George."

"That's your hard luck," the attendant informed. He tossed the cash into the till and turned to rearranging the back shelves.

At exactly eight o'clock Bransome rang the bell at the side door. Henderson answered promptly, showed him into a living room, and indicated an overstuffed chair. Blank-faced and wary, Henderson took a seat himself, lit a cigarette and spoke first.

99

"Let me tell you, Bransome, that I've heard the tune before. It's been played over two or three times for my special benefit and I'm pretty damn sick of it." He squirted a thin stream of smoke and watched it dissipate. " 'Your work at the defense plant brought you so much per annum, a nice, round, fat sum. Is this crummy store bringing you as much? What's so fascinating about the hardware trade as compared with scientific research? What's your *real* reason for swapping one for the other?' " He paused again, then said, "Right?"

"Wrong," said Bransome. "I don't care a cuss if you see fit to run a chain of brothels."

"That's a pleasant change," commented Henderson, cynically. "So they've decided to try to get at me from a different angle, eh?"

"I haven't come here to get at you."

"Then what's the idea?"

"I'm in plenty of trouble myself. I believe that you can help me quite a lot."

"Any reason why I—"

"And," interrupted Bransome, "I suspect that I can help you equally as much."

"Don't need help," Henderson asserted. "All I want is peace and a quiet life."

"So do I—but I'm not getting it." Bransome pointed a finger by way of emphasis. "Neither are you."

"That's for me to decide."

"I wouldn't dream of disputing your rights in that respect. What I'm trying to say is that I haven't got the peace of mind I'd like to have and ought to have. I don't believe you've got it either. We may be able to get it if we work together. Want to hear my story?"

"You might as well tell it now you're here. But don't start subjecting me to this come-home-all-is-forgiven stuff. I've developed a strong resistance to arguments against doing as I darned well please."

"You're still suspicious of me," said Bransome, "and I can't blame you for it. By the time I've finished you may have changed your outlook. Now listen to what I'll tell you."

He began with, "Henny, we are both scientists, you

100

of one kind and I of another. We both know that an essential attribute of a scientist, or of any technologically competent individual, is a good memory. Without it we could not have been adequately educated in the first place. Without it we could not draw data from knowledge and experience as an aid toward solving current problems. To us and those like us a good reliable memory is an absolute must. Do you agree?"

"It's too obvious to be worth mentioning," remarked Henderson, unimpressed. "I hope you are leading up to something more weighty than a mere lecture."

"I certainly am. Be patient with me. To continue: my memory always has been excellent, as it had to be to enable me to become a specialist in my field. I've learned to make full use of it, to rely upon it at all times. No doubt the same applies to you."

"No doubt," agreed Henderson, looking bored.

"Now let me tell you something else. I'm a killer. About twenty years ago I murdered a girl in a moment of temper and callously dismissed the deed from my mind. I swept it under a mental carpet because I did not want to be chivvied by the recollection of it. Recently I heard that at long last the crime has been discovered. That means the police are looking into the matter. I'm two decades ahead of them, but crimes older than mine have been solved. If the cops don't want me yet, they will before long. I'm on the run, Henny, because I don't want to be caught; I don't want to face execution at worst or a life sentence at best."

Staring at him disbelievingly, Henderson said, "You mean to tell me you're a real, genuine murderer?"

"So my good, reliable memory insists." Bransome waited to let those words sink in, then topped them devastatingly with, "My memory is a goddamned liar."

The half-smoked cigarette dropped from Henderson's fingers. He leaned sideways to snatch it from the carpet, made a couple of grabs and got it. Then he was about to put its glowing tip between his lips when he noticed it, reversed it and sucked deeply. The smoke went down the wrong way, and he had a brief fit of coughing, then recovered his breath.

"Let's get this straight, Bransome. Are you or are you not guilty of murder?"

101

"My memory says I am. It says so in clear details amounting to total recall. Even now I can see that girl's angry face as we yelled at each other. I can see the shocked stupefaction when I bashed her on the skull. I can see the loss of color in her complexion when she was lying flat and going cold. I can see the dead disinterest in her face as I smothered it under a load of dirt. The whole scene is still with me. It is as fresh and photographic as if it happened only a week or two ago. Maybe it *did* happen a week or two ago."

"What the blazes are you getting at? You've just told me you did it twenty years back."

"So my memory says. I'm telling you again that my memory is a clever and persuasive liar."

"How do you know that?"

"The facts contradict it. The lack of facts likewise. Jointly they say I've never committed such a crime."

"What facts?" demanded Henderson, trying but failing to conceal his rising interest.

"I got the willies and ran away. I was scared, really scared. I bolted—perhaps in the irrational belief that it's harder to hit a moving target." Bransome gave a rueful smile. "I could have run anywhere so long as it made me more difficult to find. For some reason I cannot explain, I did what criminals are reputed to do but probably don't—I returned to the scene of the crime."

"Ah!" Henderson stubbed out his cigarette, leaned forward with his full attention on the other. "What then?"

"I could find no evidence of it."

"None?"

"None whatever. I killed that girl outside of a small country town called Burleston. Do you know that place?"

"No, I don't."

Bransome found this answer disappointing. He continued, "I went to Burleston and questioned residents who'd spent their lives in that area. They knew nothing about any recently discovered murder. I toured the countryside seeking the spot marked X and couldn't find it or anything resembling it. I raked through past issues of the local newspaper, going back a full year, and could find no mention of an old killing coming to light."

"Perhaps you went to the wrong Burleston," Henderson suggested.

"I thought of that myself and had a look through the almanac. There is one and only one Burleston."

"Well, maybe you got the name wrong. Maybe it's some other place with a similar-sounding name."

"My memory says it's Burleston and no other."

Henderson pondered a short while then offered, "By the looks of it your memory is shot to hell."

"Dead right!" said Bransome. *"Is yours?"*

Coming swiftly to his feet, Henderson rasped, "What d'you mean, is mine?"

"Don't get agitated about it. Tell me something. Do you remember a girl named Arline Lafarge?"

"Never heard of her, and that's the truth, Bransome." Henderson started pacing to and fro across the room, his hands clasped behind his back, a look of concentration on his heavy features. He was visibly uneasy. "Is this the female you think you bumped off?"

"Yes."

"Then why should I know of her?"

"I was hoping you'd admit to killing her, too," said Bransome, evenly. "It would have been an eye-opener for both of us. We could have looked into the question of how we got that way and how best to share the grief." He watched Henderson speculatively as that person continued to parade back and forth like a restless animal. There was momentary silence which Bransome broke with, "Who did *you* kill, Henny?"

"Are you crazy?" asked Henderson, stopping in his tracks.

"Quite possibly. If so, I'm far from being the only one. A number of fellows have left the plant in circumstances that are mysterious to say the least. I've had it on good authority that other plants have lost personnel too. Nobody knows or can imagine the real reasons why they went. I couldn't have made a useful guess myself. But today is different. I am one of the departees and I *know* why I've played the frightened rabbit. Each and every man knows his secret reasons for hiding away, and each is ignorant of the other fellows' reasons. Some don't even know that there are other fugitives."

"I do," said Henderson, still punishing the carpet. "I was there when some of them left."

Bransome went on, "I checked back on myself, God alone knows why. Maybe I'm more suspicious than some. Or perhaps the delusion did not take as strong a hold on me. Besides, I'd no hole into which to crawl and couldn't think of anything better to do. So, whatever the reason may be, I went to Burleston. The result is that I'm stuck with a murder that appears never to have been committed."

"What's all this to me?"

"If all the absentees have been got on the run in the same way as I've been persuaded to bolt," Bransome explained, "I think it would be a good thing if they took time off to return to the scenes of their crimes and try to prove their own guilt. What they find—or don't find—may make their hair stand on end. And it would be a big help in getting to the bottom of this matter if they could make contact with each other and compare notes."

"That's why you've come to see me?"

"Yes."

"Have you traced any of the others?"

"No, I have not. They've vanished into the never-never. I got a lead to your lurking-place only by sheer luck. I figured it provided an opportunity too good to miss—but it won't do me anything worthwhile unless there's complete frankness on both sides."

"The approach was yours, not mine."

"I know. I've given you my reasons. I'm also giving you some excellent advice and that's this: if you have anything on your conscience, you'd do well to check on whether it really exists. I'll bet ten to one that it doesn't exist no matter how insistently your brain argues to the contrary."

"I don't regard your own checking as sufficient," Henderson opined. "On your own account it's been perfunctory. If I were in your shoes I'd want something more conclusive. After all, you've been looking for proof that you're nuts—on the principle that it's bet-

104

ter to be insane than guilty. For myself, I'd want solid evidence to satisfy me that I'm off my head."

"Couldn't agree more," Bransome told him. "Tomorrow I intend to clinch the matter one way or the other."

"How?"

"I'm going to put it to the police."

"You mean give yourself up?"

"Not on your life! I'll admit defeat when I have to and not before. I intend to call the cops long distance and sound them out. If they show no interest and prove to be as ignorant as everyone else, that'll settle it. I shall then be satisfied that, as you've suggested, I'm crazy."

"And then?"

"I can't let it rest at that. A man would be a fool to resign himself to that state of affairs. I shall have to look into the question of what has addled my brains and, if possible, do something about it. I don't want to acquire yet another nightmare at some time in the future."

"That's logical enough." Henderson gave up his restless trudging, sat down, helped himself to another cigarette. His smoking was a nervous mannerism rather than a pleasure. He eyed his visitor doubtfully. "Let's assume for the sake of argument that you're as innocent as the babe unborn. You want to find out how you became burdened with a delusion. How will you go about it? Do you know where to start looking?"

"Yes—back home. It was there I first got the jitters."

"Right in your own house?"

"No, I wouldn't say that. In my house or in the plant or somewhere between the two. Somewhere in that area. The only alternative source of information is Burleston, and if the police there know nothing about it—"

"All right. So you've an approximate idea of *where* to look—but *what* are you going to look for?"

"At the moment I haven't the remotest notion," Bransome confessed. "If the Burleston police clear me I shall go back convinced that in the home area there's

105

something to be found if only I can find it. I'm not a professional investigator nor an Indian tracker nor a smeller-out of witches. I'll have no choice but to work by guess or by God."

Henderson digested this and said after a time, "I wish Myerscough were here."

"Who's he?"

"Fellow I know. Works for the Department of Bacteriological Warfare. I've heard some strange rumors about what goes on there. It's said they've developed some kind of hell-brew that can drive people up the wall. Maybe a virus has broken loose. Maybe something's floating around that he'd recognize. If so, he could tell us."

"*Us?*" echoed Bransome, pouncing on it.

"It's your problem, but we're both discussing it, aren't we?" Henderson evaded.

"Yes, we are. And it's getting us nowhere. And I know why."

"Tell me why."

"You've been picked on already and you don't like it one little bit. So you're cagy. You don't want to trust your own shadow any farther than you can throw it. Right at the beginning you practically accused me of letting myself be used to get at you from some other and more persuasive angle."

"Well, Bransome, I'm entitled to keep—"

"You've something to hide and you're determined to play safe as long as possible by continuing to hide it. No doubt you are genuinely interested in my story. No doubt you are willing to sympathize with me on the assumption that the story may be true. But that's as far as you'll go because you can't be certain that the story is true. It could be a cunning piece of bait designed to make you blab. You're not going to allow interest or sympathy to make you blab."

"Now look here—"

"Listen to me," ordered Bransome, firmly. "Let us suppose that you're in the same fix as I am but the hallucination embedded itself more deeply in your case and you haven't undermined it by back-checking. Obviously you aren't going to ask for trouble by confessing the crime and naming the victim. Your every inclina-

106

tion will be against it. From your point of view such stupidity would enable the powers-that-be to dig up the evidence with which to convict you."

"But—"

"However, suppose you were to tell me in confidence that at some unspecified time in the past, somewhere or other, you murdered somebody or other—or believe that you did. And suppose I promptly take this information to the police. Know what they'll do? They'll welcome me with broad, anticipatory smiles. They'll find me a comfortable chair and give me coffee. They'll get all set for the coming revelation. Then they'll want to know when, where, how and who. I'll admit I can't tell them. They'll snatch away the chair and the coffee and heave me through the front door. If in a mad moment of zeal they come along to question you, what will you say? You'll deny everything and tell them I'm a nut-case. The police won't be able to take it any further and won't want to. They've more than enough to do without wasting time on useless gab."

Henderson rubbed his chin, scratched his head, fidgeted about and looked troubled. "What d'you expect me to say in reply to that homily?"

"I don't want names, dates or any other damning details. You can keep those to yourself. I want blunt and truthful replies to two blunt questions. First, do you honestly believe that you have murdered someone? Second, have you found or attempted to find any evidence in support of that belief?"

After a long pause the other said, "Yes and no."

EIGHT:

Bransome stood up and commented, "That's all I wanted to hear. It's hell to be in a boat floating on a sea of illusion. It's some comfort to know that somebody else is in the same boat. How do *you* feel about it?"

"Much as you do."

"Pity we can't get hold of the others. Between the two of us we might persuade them to talk. Then the whole bunch of us could make a joint effort to discover what has afflicted our skulls." He looked around the room. "I want my hat and coat."

"Are you going?"

"Yes. The party's over. Must go sometime."

"Where to at this ungodly hour?"

"I'll find somewhere. At the worst I can snooze in the station waiting-room."

"Didn't you come by car?"

"No—I left it with the wife."

"You're not in the big metropolis here," Henderson reminded. "You're deep in the woods. There won't be a train before ten-thirty in the morning. Why not stay here? I've got a spare bed."

"That's very kind. Sure I won't be imposing?"

"Not at all. Be glad of your company. We have something in common—if only mental deficiency."

"You have spoken sooth." Resuming his seat, Bransome gave the other a quizzical look. "What are you going to do about it?"

"I know I must do something. I can't understand why it didn't occur to me to check back in the first place, as you have done. I should have thought of it immediately but I did not. My only impulse was to get lost."

"One good reason may be that you had a hiding-place in mind whereas I hadn't," Bransome suggested. "I was at my wit's end where to go for the best. About the only out-of-the-way dump I could think of was Burleston. I went there mainly from sheer inability to imagine anywhere else." He had another thought and added, "Perhaps I was more scared than you, too scared to figure out a better move."

"I doubt it. You're not the go-haywire type. I think some small measure of incredulity was at work in your mind and urged you to go to Burleston. After all, human beings are not the same. They may react similarly —but not identically."

"I suppose so."

"To return to my own problem," Henderson went on. "I shall have to check back. That means Old Addy will have to help me out, if he's willing."

"Who's Old Addy?"

"The character who used to own this store. He splurged some of my money on a vacation, not having had one for many years. He returned about ten days ago after enjoying as good a time as one can at the age of seventy-two. Since then he's been hanging around like a lost child. Can't get used to doing nothing. A couple of times he's hinted that he's available if and when I need help. I sure could do with it if I take time off to examine my past. I've too much hard-earned money tied up in this store to neglect business even for a week or two. If Old Addy will chip in I'll be able to take a trip to—"

As Henderson's voice petered out, Bransome said, "Don't tell me. I don't want to know."

"On second thought I can't see it matters in the circumstances. After all, you've told me about Burleston."

"Yes, because I feel safer in giving forth. I've done most of my checking while you've done none. That makes all the difference. Until you satisfy yourself that you're being tormented by a fantasy, you'll be happier in the thought that I don't know enough to pin you down. So don't add to your worries after I've gone by wondering whether you've talked too much. You've got trouble enough. I know—I've had my share of it."

"Maybe you have something there," Henderson conceded.

"If you care to tell me, there's one thing I'd like to know."

"What is it?"

"Suppose you check back and discover that all is illusion—what are you going to do then? Will you enjoy your relieved conscience and remain in the hardware business? Or will you sell out and return to your former work?"

"There'll be no place for me at the plant. They'll have put someone else in my job by now. In any case, they'll have no time for characters who leave when they like and come back when they please."

"What, when they've been pestering you to return?"

"It hasn't looked that way to me. A couple of official snoops have nagged at me to give my reasons for leaving. It seemed to be the only thing that interested them. If they wanted me to return it was for further chivvying." Henderson let go a resigned sigh. "I beat them off. They got no change out of me. Soon afterward I moved here and I haven't been bothered since. I made up my mind that if they traced me and harassed me yet again, my next move would be over the border."

"That's where most of the others have gone."

"I know."

"Wish we could find and talk to them," said Bransome for the second time. He toyed with the notion of telling Henderson that already he had been traced and that a sly watch was being kept upon him, but after brief thought he dismissed the idea as something that would create unnecessary alarm and serve no useful purpose. So he continued, "What you do in the future is strictly your own affair. However, I think we should keep in touch."

"So do I."

"How about my phoning you here now and again? If you make another move you can find some way of advising me how to regain contact. I'd like to learn the result of your checking and you'll want to know about mine. One of us may stumble over something particularly enlightening to the other. We lunatics must stick together if we want to avoid being locked up."

110

"I couldn't agree more. Call me any time you like. Similarly I'll phone your home if and when I've something to say worth saying." Henderson threw a glance at the clock. "How about us turning in?"

"I'm ready." Bransome got up, stretched, yawned. "Tomorrow the police. I should have baited them in Burleston but I lacked the nerve. You must have given me some courage."

"You've given me plenty," said Henderson. "It's a fair swap."

In the morning Henderson wanted to go to the station and see his visitor depart. Bransome discouraged the idea.

"Let's not draw even casual attention to ourselves. You preside in the store and I'll walk out looking like a satisfied customer."

They shook hands and parted. Outside, Bransome glanced around in search of Reardon's watcher. The only suspect he could find was a scruffy idler on the near corner. This character eyed him dully as he brushed past. Farther along the street, Bransome looked back. The idler was still on the corner and making no attempt to follow. Either the supposed watch on Henderson's place was a half-hearted, sloppy job or, perhaps, too expert to be detected.

He was not joined on the train by anyone he could deem suspicious. The journey involved a change at one point, with a half-hour wait. He filled in his time at the latter by finding a phone booth and calling the Hanbury police. When a voice responded he asked for the chief. The voice became curious, and showed an officious tendency to argue the request until Bransome became tough and threatened to hang up. At that point he was switched through.

"Chief Pascoe," announced a deeper and gruffer voice. "Who's calling?"

"My name is Robert Lafarge," said Bransome, glibly. "About twenty years ago my sister Arline went on a visit to Burleston and never returned. We had reason to believe that she'd run off with a man or something like that—you know, a secret romance. She always had been a wayward and impulsive character."

"What's all this to me?" asked Chief Pascoe, patiently.

"Not known! Not known!" shouted eerily in Bransome's brain. It had a touch of triumph.

He continued, "Recently I've been talking to a fellow from your town. He mentioned that some time ago—I don't know exactly when—you had found the bones of a girl buried under a tree. The discovery was obvious evidence of an old crime, according to him. It got me worried. I wondered if the victim could be Arline and whether you'd found any evidence in support."

"Who is this informant? A friend of yours?"

"No, sir—just a casual acquaintance."

"You're sure he said Hanbury?"

"He said it was just outside Burleston. That's in your jurisdiction, isn't it?"

"Certainly is. And if such a thing had happened we'd know of it. We don't know of it."

"You mean—"

"We've unearthed no bones, Mr. Lafarge. Have you any good reason to suspect that your sister met with foul play?"

"Afraid I haven't. It's only that we haven't heard from her in years, and this story sort of made me put two and two together."

"Did your informant know about your sister?"

"Not a thing."

"You said nothing to him about her?"

"Definitely not."

"Then he's given you a figment of his imagination."

"That may be so," Bransome conceded, noticing that the other was making no attempt to hold him on the line long enough to make a pickup. "But I see no point in it. He had nothing to gain by feeding me a fairy story."

"He gained a listener," retorted Chief Pascoe, sounding cynical. "A yap needs a listener like a drug addict needs a shot in the arm. That's why every once in a while we get people confessing to crimes they didn't commit and begging us to take them in. It would be a good thing if there were bigger penalties for being a public nuisance. We get more than enough of our time wasted as it is."

112

"So you don't think it's any use my coming there to have a look around?" asked Bransome, knowing full well that Pascoe would make unhesitating use of his willingness to enter the trap—if a trap actually existed.

"There's nothing for you to see, Mr. Lafarge."

"Thanks!" said Bransome, vastly relieved. "Genuinely sorry to have troubled you."

"Think nothing of it. You took the proper action in the circumstances. Our best leads come from people with suspicions, but yours have no basis so far as we are concerned. That's all we're able to say."

Bransome thanked him again and ended the call. Leaving the booth, he sat on a nearby bench and thought things over. He was baffled. So far as one can judge a voice without actually seeing the speaker, Chief Pascoe was sincere and forthright. He had not tried to hold his caller while an aide got the local police racing to the booth; that would have been his obvious tactic when saddled with an unsolved murder and in telephone contact with a suspect.

He'd even turned down Bransome's offer to stick his head in the lion's mouth. That clinched the matter—there had not been any gruesome exhumation in Burleston despite that Bransome's memory made it possible and despite the trucker's statement that it had been done.

The easiest and most enticing solution of this puzzle lay in the theory already considered and rejected a dozen times, namely, that the trucker had talked about some other remarkably similar crime and thus unwittingly had awakened Bransome's guilty conscience. But the idea had several flaws. While it might explain his own panic-stricken gallivantings, it did not explain Henderson's. It did not rationalize Reardon's activities or those of the mysterious big man thought by Dorothy to be a foreigner.

Even Reardon's own explanations did not fully fit the peculiar circumstances. According to him the country's various defense establishments had lost a number of good men and at that time he was keeping tab on two of them, one of whom was Bransome. How could one account for all the others—in terms of a gabby trucker?

What was it Reardon had said? The company may become a regiment and the regiment an army—if we don't stop it. Stop *what?* Answer: whatever it is that makes intelligent men seek a hiding-place. All these men were scientists, or high-grade specialists of some sort, and therefore of the calm, logical and somewhat unemotional type least likely to go off the rails. What could unbalance men like that?

He could imagine only one thing. Fear of death.

Any kind of death—especially judicial execution.

The train came in and he got himself an isolated seat where he could handle his problems in peace. For the moment he was only dimly aware of the existence of other passengers and little concerned about whether any were interested in him.

Thought was a good deal more orderly and systematic now that a hefty slice of his emotional disturbance had been removed. He felt as if an invisible hand had been thrust into his skull and taken away a cluster of impeding marbles that had been rolling around too confusingly and too long. One or two remained, but they weren't of the heart-straining, sweat-making variety. His guilt persisted to some extent but was no longer fitted with a clamorous alarm-bell; Chief Pascoe had snatched away that distracting accessory and tossed it on the junkpile. For the first time in days he could sit and listen to his own thinking processes.

Firstly, Arline, real or imaginary, was still down wherever he'd put her and with luck would remain there until the crack of doom. From his personal point of view that was item number one, the most important of the lot. The police did not want him, did not suspect him, did not care a hoot about him or the murky episode in his past. The death-chamber did not have his name upon it; if it was being held in readiness it was for another who, no doubt, was viewing it in his dreams exactly as Bransome had done.

Secondly, he was being chivvied by groups other than the police for an unknown something of lesser consequence—because any misdeed is of consequence

114

lesser than the one that carries the capital penalty. Alternatively, he was being chased for something he had not yet done but was considered capable of doing and likely to do.

It was nothing he'd done already, of that he was sure. Positively and beyond all doubt Arline monopolized the only dark space in his mind. There was no other guilt, nothing with which to reproach himself.

So it must be a future crime, the possibility if not the probability of what he might yet do. In his special position there were only two things he could do to outrage the powers-that-be: he could go over to the enemy or at least desert his own side. This was what bothered Reardon, who had said so in plain terms. It wasn't flattering. It implied that both sides, friend and foe, had weighed him up as a weak sister. Both sides recognized him as an easy mark, a sucker.

He scowled at the thought of it. Other people's opinions of him must be pretty low if it was apparent to all and sundry that he was an open chink in his country's armor. They wouldn't pick on hard, taciturn men like Markham, Cain, Potter and several more. Oh, no, they'd just naturally go for a soft touch like Richard Bransome who needed no more than a gentle shove.

Becoming emotional again, he thought. Men tend to get that way when they think their self-esteem is being kicked around. Ego is dangerously diversionary and misleading. It must not be taken into consideration. Let's look at things objectively.

Why should an enemy select me as a suitable target in preference to others? Answer: their tactics are determined by expediency and they choose the target available at a given moment in given circumstances. Then when am I peculiarly suitable? Answer: when the enemy is ready and I am immediately available while others are not. I represent an opportunity. Why does Joe Soap get knocked down by a car while none of his friends and neighbors suffer the same tragedy? Answer: because Joe and the car created the event by coinciding in time and space.

Knocked down?

Knocked down?

His fingers curled into a tight grip while his eyes

115

expressed startlement. That evil day had begun with an inexplicable tumble down the steps. In his mind's eye he could see himself right now doing it all over again. Descending the first ten or twelve steps with forty more waiting below. Then the flash of light and the headlong, neck-breaking dive from which he'd been saved only by two men on their way up. He could picture vividly their outstretched arms, their anticipatory faces as he plunged down upon them.

Their hands had grabbed him a split second before he'd hit and had saved him from crashing the whole way down. Now that he came to think of it, he realized they'd been amazingly swift to sum up the situation and do something about it, almost as if they had known what was about to happen and been ready to play their part. They'd reacted with all the promptitude of men blessed with prevision, and that alone had saved him from serious injury.

Nevertheless, he had banged himself around more than he'd cared to admit to Dorothy. He had knocked himself out and regained consciousness sitting midway down the steps with his two catchers tending to him and showing plausible concern. The big bruise on his elbow was understandable because he could remember striking it upon a concrete step just before he'd passed out. The blow on the skull and the large bump it raised were something else again; he had no recollection of that injury in the making.

Holy smoke, could he have been slugged from behind?

At that time the incident had shaken him mentally and physically to such an extent that his work-free morning had been hopelessly muddled. Recapturing it now, he could not recall what he'd done with the rest of his time before reaching the plant at mid-day. He had worried about the mental blackout that had either accompanied or caused his fall, had wondered if his heart were acting up and whether he had better consult a doctor at risk of being told the worst.

Yes, his subsequent confusion had been so great that temporarily he had lost all sense of time. Somehow or other two hours had disappeared out of his morning, he'd suddenly found it far later than he thought, and he'd had to take a taxi to reach the plant by deadline.

And so had commenced Friday the Thirteenth.

His unlucky day. A fall. Two men ready to catch him. A bump on the skull from nowhere. Time missing from his morning. A pair of truckers gossiping within earshot and giving him the heebies. The big man following him around. The flight of a frightened rat. Reardon on the trail. A company, a regiment, an army.

He sat taut in his seat as inexorably his mind carried its thoughts along. It takes arduous and careful preparation to make an atomic bomb after which the contraption is of no use except potentially.

"It doesn't mean a thing if you don't pull the string."

Suppose, just suppose that one could apply a somewhat similar technique to the human mind, adding to its data-banks an item large enough to create critical mass. The brain would remain at rest until it and the new part were brought forcibly together. It could be left in peace, maybe for weeks or months, until the moment arrived to trigger the situation thus set up.

A few words spoken by a mock-trucker.

The detonating mechanism.

Mental explosion!

He came out of the railroad station in a hell of a hurry, brushing passers-by, bumping into one or two and throwing them a muttered apology. Several people turned to stare after him. He was aware of their scrutiny and knew that he was making himself conspicuous but was too absorbed in himself to care.

The real solution of his predicament lay with the company that might become a regiment. He knew that as surely as he knew the difficulty of finding and pinning down the company. Some of them could tell him what had given them the willies; some might be less cautious and more candid than the not-too-helpful Henderson. Any few would do provided that they could be induced to open their minds to another nightmare-addict.

"Look, brother, I'm not a cop, I'm not a security

117

agent, I'm not a stooge of authority. I'm Richard Bransome, a fellow research worker on the run from everybody because I'm in a dream-world of my own. I'm not wanted for a murder that I believe I've committed. I'm convinced that in the long ago I killed a girl named Arline Lafarge. What do you think *you've* done?"

If only one of them, just one would say, "My God, Bransome, there's something screwy here. I killed Arline myself, near a one-horse dump called Burleston. I know I did it. How the devil could you—"

"Tell me why you did it."

"She was a bitch. She drove me to it. I did it in a blazing temper. She got me really mad."

"How?"

"Well . . . uh . . . I just don't recall right now. It was so long ago and I've tried hard to forget it."

"Same with me. How about us tracking down the others and finding how many more have bumped Arline? It would be nice to know. We could present the cops with a mass-confession and squat in jail together and count the hours to the end."

Might it work out that way? Nothing the human mind can conceive is impossible. On the other hand, unknown forces might have been too farseeing and crafty for such simplification and taken the precaution of burdening each victim with a different phantom. Henderson, for example, appeared to have a secret peculiarly his own; he had not blinked an eyelid at mention of Burleston and Arline and had denied knowing either place or person.

He was commencing to feel pretty positive that the ill-fated Arline was an illusionary creature. It was hard, very hard to accept this idea because his memory persisted in contradicting it. To deny the dictates of his memory was about as difficult as it would be to repudiate his own face in the mirror.

In spite of accumulating evidence and/or lack of evidence, in spite of rapidly growing doubts, his memory remained sharp and clear with respect to the worst moment of his life. Even though the vision of the past might be no more than a bad dream built around a ghostly female, he could still visualize Arline's features as she went down to her death, her black hair tied with baby-blue ribbon at the nape of her neck, her jet-black eyes full of shock, her thin lips that had curled in scorn once too often, the faint freckles on the sides of her nose, the streak of blood creeping down her forehead. She had been wearing a string of graduated pearls with button earrings to match, a blue dress, black shoes, a gold wristwatch. The picture was stereoscopic and in full color even to her nail-polish, which was lurid. It was a vision as complete in detail as only a reproduction of the real can be complete.

But was she real?

Or was she a mental figment just sufficiently large to create critical mass?

The other refugees would know all about her or about phantoms like her. It would be hard if not impossible to get at them without Reardon's co-operation. He did not fancy seeking Reardon's help, especially after recent events. Besides, such a move would get him all tied up in bureaucratic complications at the very time when he was about to switch from the hunted to the hunter. He would appeal to Reardon and the redoubtable forces behind him only at the last resort.

Therefore his fellow fugitives could be of no help in raising the pursuit, though, with luck, Henderson might prove a slow and stodgy exception. For the time being he'd have to run along on his own—and, he decided, there *was* a quarry to be tracked down.

Five men could solve the mystery of Arline Lafarge. Five knew all about her and could be forced to talk.

Those five were the two who had grabbed him on the steps, also the talkative trucker and his stooge, also the big foreigner who had egged him into flight. If he were right in these conclusions there was a sixth man, the unseen slugger, whom he could not include in his calculations because he had no means of identifying him.

Any one of the five could give a lead to the others and, perhaps, to a bigger mob lurking in the background.

As he hastened along he amused himself by making a more or less impassive study of his thirst for vengeance. Being what he was, primarily an objective thinker, he'd always viewed as a symptom of primitivism the supreme delight of handing someone a bust on the nose. Now the desire didn't seem so retrogressive. Indeed he'd have despised himself had he lacked it. One cannot dispense with everything, basic human feelings included. He was happily married and that sweet state could never have been attained without emotional qualities on his part.

Yes, if the opportunity came along, or if somehow he could create the chance, he was going to build up pressure of emotion to the bursting point, force all of it down into his right fist and make a hell of a mess of somebody's face.

In other words, he was riled and enjoying it.

NINE:

NIGHT'S DARK curtain lay across the sky, street lamps were gleaming, shop-fronts lit up. This was his own town but he did not go home; if anyone wanted him it was there they'd keep watch, waiting for the lost sheep to return to the fold. So far as he was concerned, they could wait until they took root. He had no hankering to be picked up yet. What he needed more than anything else was time—time enough to prowl around, find a target for his ire and dish out some hefty punches.

His progress through town was fast but careful. A hundred people, some of them workers at the plant, lived hereabouts and knew him if only by sight. He didn't want to be seen, much less spoken to, by any of them. The less others knew about his return, the better. Using the darker streets and avoiding the main shopping areas, he stopped only at a small store to buy himself a razor, toothbrush and comb. His journey ended at a motel on the side of town farthest from his house.

There he cleaned up and had a meal. For a short while he suffered the temptation to phone Dorothy and arrange to meet her at a roadside cafe or some such place. But the children soon would be going to bed and she'd have to find a neighbor willing to baby-sit. The morning would be better, after the kids had gone to school. In the meantime he could have a word with Henderson if that worthy were still at Lakeside. He put through the call and Henderson answered.

"You still there? I thought you might have left by now."

"I'm going tomorrow afternoon," Henderson informed. "Old Addy's taking over for a short time and is delighted to do so. Don't know why he sold the store in the first place. Did you bait the you-know-who?"

"Yes. There was nothing doing."

"What d'you mean?"

"They know nothing about it, and that's definite."

Henderson was doubtful. "If they did know something, they wouldn't necessarily admit it to an unknown voice on the phone. More likely they'd have tried to pick you up. Did you give them enough time to make a grab?"

"No, I didn't."

"In that case you can't take anything for granted."

"I didn't need to give them time. They weren't trying to pick me up."

"How can you be sure of that?"

"Because they made no attempt to detain me on the line," explained Bransome. "Furthermore, I offered to go see them and they wouldn't take me up on it. They said it would be a waste of time. They weren't the least bit interested in seeing me, never mind making a grab. I'm telling you, Henny, the whole affair is some kind of dope-dream and I'm proceedig on that assumption."

"Proceeding? What can you do about it? D'you mean you're returning to the plant?"

"No—I'm not going back to work just yet."

"Then what?"

"I'm determined to do some smelling around. With luck I might discover something worth finding. At any rate, I'm going to have a try. Nothing ventured, nothing gained."

"You've got a lead worth following?"

"I may have. I can't be sure about it right now." Bransome frowned to himself and went on, "If, as I expect, your own queries really satisfied you that your worries are baseless, I suggest you think back to the circumstances in which they started. You should be able to remember the people who shared those circumstances. They are your suspects. See what I mean?"

"Bransome," said Henderson, unimpressed, "you may fancy yourself as a private investigator, but I'm no detective and I know it. I'm not suited to that kind of work either by training or by inclination."

"I'm no better suited, but that won't stop me. You never know what you can do until you try."

"Have it your own way."

"I intend to. I'm sick and tired of having it in somebody else's way." He clenched a fist and eyed it as if it were symbolic. "Henny, if you find you're in the clear, for Pete's sake don't rest content to leave it at that. Don't settle down to be happy and let sleeping dogs lie. Come back here and join forces with me. We may have been hexed by the same bunch of characters. You might recognize one and me another. We could help each other to pin them down."

"I'm not committing myself just yet," said Henderson, instinctively countering yet another come-home-all-is-forgiven gambit. "You've checked and you're looking for blood. I'm about to check and I'm hoping for salvation. At the present moment our positions are very different. In a few days' time I may have moved over to your position. I may then be ripe for mayhem —in which case I'll decide what to do for the best."

"You won't be human if you don't want to subject someone to the death of a thousand cuts," Bransome opined. "You'll need a helper to hold the victim down. I'm applying in advance for that job. You can reciprocate by doing the same for me."

"I'll let you know how I get on," Henderson promised.

"Best of luck!"

Ending the call, Bransome borrowed one of the motel's telephone directories, took it to his room, and spent an hour searching through it and making notes. He finished with a short list containing the addresses and phone numbers of a legal advisory service, a mental specialist, a car rental agency, two detective outfits, four trucking companies and several modest eating places that he had never frequented. Most of this data might not be used but it would be convenient to have it ready to hand. Shoving the list into his wallet, he prepared for bed. His sleep that night was deep and untroubled.

At nine-thirty in the morning, estimating that by now she would have returned from taking the children to school, he phoned Dorothy. He was careful about arranging to see her; she would be a direct lead to him, there was no knowing who might be listening on the line or who might be glad to learn of the rendezvous.

"Listen, Lovely, this is urgent and I mustn't waste words. So let's keep it short, eh? Can you meet me for lunch about twelve-thirty?"

"Of course, Rich, I'll be quite—"

"Remember where you lost and found your silver compact? I'll wait for you there."

"Yes, all right, but why do—"

He hung up as she was speaking. No doubt she'd feel irked about that, but it couldn't be helped. Reardon and those behind him had the power to tap a telephone line and, in his opinion, weren't above doing it for five cents. Brevity and evasiveness were the only defenses against an eavesdropper.

By ten o'clock he was loafing around the gates of a trucking company. This was in the industrial district, a broad road lined with factories, yards and warehouses. Traffic was sparser than in the center of town, almost all of it consisting of huge vehicles bearing heavy loads. Pedestrians were so few that he was conspicuous and painfully aware of it. Undeterred, he strolled to and fro by the gates for an hour and a half during which time one truck entered and none emerged. He got a good look at the driver and co-driver. Both were complete strangers.

Just inside the gates was a weighing station, alongside it a small hut inhabited by another watcher who wrote something in a book as the truck lumbered through, then gazed boredly through the window. He began to notice Bransome's occasional amblings past the gates and eyed him with increasing curiosity. Eventually he left his hut and came outside.

"Waiting for someone, mister?"

"I'm looking for a couple of fellows I know," said Bransome, laconically.

"Truckers?"

"Yes."

"Kept you long enough, haven't they? Give me their names and I'll tell 'em you're here."

124

"Sorry, I can't—I know them only by sight."

"That's a big help," commented the other. A phone shrilled in the hut. "Hold it a minute." He dashed into the hut, answered, consulted his book and transmitted some information. Then he returned to the gates.

"I can describe them," said Bransome.

"That's a fat lot of use. I'm no good at that sort of thing. Couldn't recognize my Aunt Martha if you painted her on oils."

"Be surprised if you could—the way I paint."

"You couldn't be worse than me, mister." He scratched his bristly head, pondered the problem, then pointed across the yard. "Go into that office over there and ask for Richards. He knows every employee like he knows his own face. He ought to—he hires 'em and fires 'em."

"Thanks a lot." Bransome trudged across the yard, entered the office, and said to the girl behind the counter, "Can I have a word with Mr. Richards, please?"

She looked him over with cool calculation. "You looking for a job?"

"No," said Bransome, deeply shocked. "I'm seeking some information."

Richards came after a few minutes. He was a thin-featured, disillusioned-looking type. His voice suggested patience that came with effort.

"Can I help you?"

"I hope so. I'm trying to find a couple of truckers."

"What for?"

"Eh?"

"What d'you want 'em for? Are they in trouble of some kind? Who are you anyway? A cop or an insurance investigator?"

"Seems to me you're all set to expect the worst," said Bransome, grinning. "You must have plenty of woe from truckers."

"That's my business. What's yours?"

Since the other seemed accustomed to dealing only with authority, any kind of authority, Bransome gave him a half-truth. "I'm an official from the Defense Department." He exhibited his pass and noted that it was examined with gratifying respect. "I have reason to

125

believe that two truckers can supply some information of interest to the department. If I can find them I'd like to ask them a few questions."

Now satisfied, Richards said less surlily, "What are their names?"

"I don't know. I can give their descriptions. Your gateman thinks you might be able to identify them for me."

"All right, I'll try. What do they look like?"

Bransome provided verbal pictures of the pair of gossipers in the diner. He flattered himself that they were very good descriptions given in full detail.

When he had finished Richards said, "We have forty-eight assorted roughnecks driving all over the country. About twenty of them correspond more or less with the idea you've given of the men you want. Some won't be back for a couple of days, others for a week or more. If you want to have a look at them, you're in for quite a long wait."

"That's bad," conceded Bransome, disappointed. "You sure they work for this outfit?"

"I don't know who they work for."

"Jumping Joseph!" Richards eyed him incredu-lously. "What kind of badges do they wear on their pocket-flaps?"

"No idea."

"Well, what kind of a truck were they using? What color was it and what lettering or symbols did it carry?"

"Don't know. When last seen they weren't in a truck. They were in the railroad station, presumably waiting for a train."

"Oh, Lord!" Richards threw an appealing glance toward heaven. "Let me tell you something. Ordinary truckers do not use trains, not unless they're being taken home for burial. They use trucks. They take loads out and they bring loads back, if and when a return-load can be got. Otherwise they come back empty. So in all probability your men are transfer-truckers."

"Huh?"

"A transfer-trucker," explained Richards with exag-gerated patience, "takes a load away and delivers it,

126

truck and all, at some distant trucking depot. He gets further orders there. Either at that depot or at some other reached by bus or train, he picks up another loaded truck, takes it away and delivers it. And so on and so on. He also acts as relief man, handling trucks for fellows on vacation or sick or thrown into the jug. He's a gypsy, a wanderer, a general messer-abouter, here today and gone tomorrow and God only knows where the day after."

"I see," said Bransome, feeling that as a detective he was proving somewhat feeble.

"The point is this: transfer-truckers are used only by the big interstate companies with a number of depots. Not by small outfits like the four in this town. There are dozens of interstaters each employing hundreds of men. All you've got is a couple of descriptions that might fit a thousand or more guys at present trundling around anywhere from the North Pole downward." He spread hands in a gesture of futility. "It's worse than looking for a couple of special fleas in a dogs' home. If I were you, I'd quit. Life's too short."

"I guess that finishes that," said Bransome, ruefully. He turned to go. "I'm grateful for what you've told me. We're never too old to learn."

"Think nothing of it." Richards watched him reach the door then called, "Hey, there's something else now that I come to think of it. A pair of transfer-truckers wouldn't be waiting at the local station."

"Why not?"

"They never come here. There isn't an interstate depot in this town."

"That means they may not have been what they appeared to be, eh? Well, I saw them myself and they certainly looked like truckers."

"In our servicing bay we've a chump who looks like Napoleon—but he isn't."

Returning to the counter, Bransome leaned across it, grasped Richards' forearm, held it up and said loudly, I declare you the winner."

He left, moodily crossed the yard and reached the exit. The gateman came out of his hut and asked, "Any luck, mister?" Bransome said, "I was too late. They're being fried tomorrow. Justice shall be done." He kept

127

127

on walking, giving no opportunity for further questions. Behind him the gateman spent a moment looking thunderstruck, then dashed into his hut and snatched up the phone. "Who's being taken and what for? Or is that fellow a nut-case?" A voice replied, "You're paid to keep 'em out, not to show 'em in. Wake up, Sweeny!"

Knowing from experience exactly what Dorothy's routine would be, Bransome stationed himself at the back of a small parking lot and observed her arrival. About five minutes before the meeting time she drove through the entrance, expertly reversed into a vacant space, got out and locked the car doors. Pausing only to feed the meter she left the park, turned to the right and sauntered along the road. Her handbag was tucked under her right arm, a familiar-looking suitcase was swinging from her left hand and she was displaying the usual long, slender legs at which various males threw appreciative glances.

Another car drove in and positioned itself not far from Dorothy's. Two men emerged, put money in the meter and turned to the right. They walked at easy pace a couple of hundred yards behind Dorothy. Ordinarily, Bransome would have felt highly suspicious of this pair, but both were elderly and silver-haired, in his opinion too old to play the professional tracker. All the same, he came from his hiding place and followed them in their turn, meanwhile keeping careful watch for any other shadowers that Dorothy might innocently be leading around.

Before long the two oldsters mounted the steps of an office building and pushed through its revolving door. Dorothy was still visible walking onward with occasional slowings in pace as she passed an interesting shop window. Keeping his eyes peeled, Bransome could find nothing to show that she was under observation. He was looking mostly for a too-casual pedestrian strolling in the same direction and it did not occur to him to watch passing traffic.

Dorothy reached the small restaurant where, years ago, she had lost and regained her compact. She went inside, being characteristically right on time. On the opposite side of the road Bransome kept going, walked a hundred yards or so farther on, crossed the street and came back. He failed to spot anyone confused by this maneuver. So far as he could tell, the coast was clear. He went into the restaurant and found her sitting expectantly at a secluded table for two.

"Hi, sweetheart!" Slinging his hat onto a nearby hook, he took the opposite chair.

"Hi, sloppy!" she greeted. "Been sleeping in your suit?"

Instinctively smoothing his sleeves, he said, "It's not that rumpled."

"What have you been sleeping in?" she asked with dangerous sweetness.

"Beds," he told her. "See here, I haven't met you just to—" He shut up as she leaned sideways, grasped the suitcase on the floor and pushed it forward slightly. It was the one that he'd abandoned on the train. He gazed at it morbidly. "How did you get it?"

"A tall, dark stranger crossed my path. He knocked at the door and gave it to me."

"Did he give you his name as well?"

"Yes—Reardon. Naturally I wanted to know how he'd come by it and what you were doing without your shaving gear and pajamas."

"If you must know, I've slept in my underwear. What did he tell you?"

"He said you were growing a beard and sleeping naked for reasons he did not care to mention. He remarked that if I asked no questions I'd be told no lies and, anyway, he wanted no hand in a possible divorce."

"Trust him to say things like that," commented Bransome. "He wants you to gab about me. No doubt he figures you'd be more willing to co-operate if you were annoyed. Did he ask a load of questions about whether you had heard from me and where I was and what I was doing and so on?"

"He did ask a few. I told him nothing. After all, there was nothing I *could* tell him." She became more serious. "What's going on, Rich?"

"I wish I could give you the full facts, but I can't.

129

Not yet, at least. When it comes to an end the authorities may want to keep it dark. You know how tough they are with people who talk too much."

"Yes, of course."

"However, I can tell you this: it's a security matter. It involves me, and that's what had me worried before I went away. I've since discovered that it affects a number of other employees as well. The big consolation is that as far as I, personally, am concerned it's not as serious as first it seemed."

"That's something," she said, openly relieved.

"But it doesn't satisfy me. For reasons I cannot explain, this thing must be seen through to the bitter end." He sought a way of making her understand without revealing anything. "It's like a decaying tooth. By dabbing it with oil of cloves I've stopped the ache and feel happier for it. However, that's only a palliative and I'd be a fool to kid myself that it's a cure. To do a proper job the tooth must be extracted."

"By you?"

"I'm one of the sufferers and I feel entitled to do something about it—if I can."

"What of the others you've mentioned? Are they incapable of taking action?"

"They've lammed out of reach and don't realize what is going on. I found—" He caught her warning look, glanced up and found a waiter standing silently by his elbow. Accepting a menu, he discussed it with Dorothy and gave their orders. The waiter went away. Bransome continued with, "I found one character who before long may be able and willing to help. Fellow named Henderson, a red-area ballistician. Remember him?"

"Can't say I do," she admitted after some thought.

"Burly type with a slight paunch, hair thinning on top, wears rimless glasses and talks like a lecturer. You met him some months ago."

"I still don't recall him. Evidently he didn't create much of an impression."

"He wouldn't. He never tries to. He's not what one would call a ladies' man."

"Meaning he keeps his paws to himself?"

"That's right. Doesn't want to get his fingers

130

trapped. He may phone at any time. I won't be home for a few days but don't let that worry you. I've good reasons for staying away."

"So this man Reardon implied."

"Damn Reardon! Now, if and when Henderson calls, tell him that I'm on the job but not immediately available and that you'll take his message. If he expects a reply, ask him if I'm to phone the store or some other number. Is that okay?"

"I'll cope. The art of marriage is coping."

"Another thing: if Reardon or that big foreigner or anyone else arrives at the house and starts pestering you with questions, you still know nothing, see? You don't know where I am or when I'll return. You've never heard of Henderson even though you've just been talking to him. Doesn't matter who the questioner may be, a reporter, an F.B.I. agent or a ten-star general in full uniform, you don't know a darned thing."

"Check," she said. "Am I permitted to know just who this Reardon is?"

"A security officer. Belongs to Military Intelligence."

She showed surprise and some puzzlement. "Then surely it's his job and not yours to—"

Bransome interrupted, "For one thing, suffering is educative and he hasn't suffered and can't be expected to understand the mentalities of those who have. For another, there are different ideas of what constitutes security. For a third, he's trained to deal with orthodox problems by orthodox methods. I don't want him tramping all over my feet, messing me up and pushing me around. There's enough regimentation in the plant without having more of it outside."

"All right, if he calls on me I'll treat him to a demonstration of wide-eyed ignorance."

"You do that. He won't be fooled for one minute—but neither will he learn anything."

The meal came. Until it was finished they resorted to idle gossip. Over coffee, Bransome came back to the subject.

"One more item. This big clunker whom you believe to be a foreigner. I've seen him a few times and know how he looks. But I'd like to have your description of

131

him. Different people notice different things and you may be able to augment my own picture of him."

Dorothy obliged in manner showing that she was very observant. To Bransome's memory of the man she added a thin white scar, about one inch long, set diagonally on the right side of the upper lip. He had a habit, she said, of pursing his lips after putting a question and it was then that the scar showed up as a crease in the flesh. Apart from that she had nothing to add except her intuitive feeling that he was a stolid but brutal type who'd be slow to lose his temper and equally slow to recover it.

"He seemed the sort of man who'd take an awful lot of provocation before he hit out—but once started he wouldn't know when to stop."

"His manner toward you wasn't tough?"

"No, not at all. He was unctuously polite."

"H'm!" His fingers tapped idly on the table as again he visualized the subject of their conversation. The waiter misunderstood his rapping and brought the bill. Bransome paid it and, after the other had gone, said to Dorothy, "During the last few days have you noticed anyone following you around?"

"No, Rich. I haven't been watching for any such thing. Do you consider it likely?"

"It's possible. Anyone wanting to find me would keep an eye on you."

"Yes, I suppose they would."

"From now on I'd like you to see if you can spot anyone tagging along behind. If you do, don't let it bother you. Try to get a close look at him so that you can describe him to me. I may be able to figure out a way of making him provide me with a lead."

"He could be another security man, couldn't he?"

"Yes. One of Reardon's bunch. But there's a chance that he might be an observer for quite a different mob, in which case he's my meat." Getting up, he reached for his hat. "Tell the kids I'll be home before long. I'll phone you tomorrow evening after they've gone to bed."

"All right." She gathered her things together and left with him. Outside she asked, "Do you need the car? Or can I drive you somewhere?"

132

"I'm better off without the car. Too many snoops know its license number. I don't want to advertise myself all over town."

She put a hand on his arm. "Rich, are you sure you know what you're doing?"

"No, I don't. I'm like a blind man fumbling in the dark and hoping to put a hand on something worth grabbing." He gave her hand a reassuring pat. "I may get nowhere, in which case I'll be happy in the thought that it wasn't for lack of trying."

"I know how you feel." With a doubtful smile she set off in the direction of the parking lot.

Watching her until she was out of sight, Bransome hailed a taxi and was taken to the office of another trucking company. He was not sanguine about the usefulness of this visit but did want authoritative confirmation of the remarks made by Richards.

They said, "Look, mister, without names or photographs you've as much chance of tracing those guys as of having a drink with the Pope. They might be anybody and they might be anywhere. What d'you expect us to do about it?"

He left the place feeling satisfied that this line of investigation was fruitless. Ergo, he'd have to try some other line. He'd admit himself beaten when he had exhausted every possibility and not before.

Walking through a series of side streets he tried to work out his plan of campaign. Were there any other paths of approach that might lead him to the truckers? He could imagine only one, that being the station snack bar where he had encountered them. Somebody who frequented the place might know the identities of those two, a railroad official or a fellow commuter or some other trucker.

If he eliminated this pair as unfindable, what other leads remained? For one, there was the big shadower who had out-stared him in the mirror, who had disappeared not far from home and therefore might be living in that neighborhood. And then there were the two unknown men who had witnessed his fall down the steps and reacted thereto. He'd seen them only hazily in the second or two before he'd collapsed, but more clearly after his recovery. Their faces remained impressed

133

upon his mind with photographic accuracy, especially the one who had been slapping his face to bring him to his senses. He felt sure that if he should encounter them again he would recognize them at once. But where to look for them? Like the vanished truckers, they might be anybody and might be anywhere.

At the last resort he had the choice of three moves. Using Dorothy as bait he could try to pick up a shadower and use him as a lead to others in the background. Or he could make another pass at Henderson in the hope that two might succeed where one had failed. Or he could treat Reardon to an hour of true confessions and leave the powers-that-be to handle things in whatever way they saw fit.

The last idea was so distasteful that automatically he rejected it, speeded up his pace and headed for the station. He did not and could not know it at the time but it was his first move in the right direction. At long last he was about to start getting somewhere.

TEN:

Marching into the snack bar long before his customary time, he eased himself onto a high stool, ordered coffee and waited until the attendant had finished serving others. When the fellow was free he gave him the nod, leaned over the counter and spoke in low tones.

"Walt, I'm looking for someone and you may be able to help me. Do you remember a couple of hefty characters in denims and peaked caps? They were in here swilling coffee a week or so ago. Looked like truck-drivers. They were talking about a murder somewhere or other."

"Murder?" Walt's eyebrows twitched. He put on the expression of one hoping for the best while expecting the worst. "No, Mr. Bransome. I heard nobody talking about anything like that. I don't remember those guys either."

"Try and think. Two truckers sitting right here."

Obediently Walt tried and thought. "Sorry, Mr. Bransome—I don't recall them at all. I ought to, if they were truckers. We don't get 'em here very often. I couldn't have taken much notice of them at the time. I don't pay much attention to casual customers unless they attract it by busting a window or fainting on the floor or something like that." Another thought struck him and he asked, "You sure I was on duty then?"

"Yes, it was a Friday evening. You're always on duty Fridays, aren't you?"

"Sure am. Maybe I was busy. I don't take a lot in when I've plenty to do. People can be talking all around me and none of it registers until they shout an order."

"Do you think you'd remember them if they'd been here a number of times?"

135

"That's likely," said Walt. "As I said, it isn't often we get truckers in here."

"So the implication is that they were here only the once and you haven't seen them since?"

"Correct."

"Well, how about another fellow? Here by himself a couple of days later. No, four or five days later. Big guy. Over six feet tall, two hundred pounds, flattened nose, florid face with heavy chops, white scar on top lip, looked like an ex-pug or maybe an older policeman in plain clothes. He sat up here right by the counter, saying nothing and staring at the mirror as if it fascinated him."

"Wears a snake-ring on his left hand?" prompted Walt, frowning to himself.

"I believe he did wear a ring of some kind, but I didn't see it close up."

"Talks like a foreigner?"

"Haven't heard him speak a word, but I've good reason to think he may be a foreigner."

"Been in here a few times." Walt glanced at the wall-clock. "Somewhere about now or perhaps a little later. Haven't seen him for a week though. I can remember him because he gave me the creeps. Always by himself, using his eyes a lot and saying nothing. Used to stare at me as if making ready to complain about something and wreck the joint. But he never got around to it."

"Know anything about him?"

"Only that I sized him up as a foreigner."

"Ever see him in the company of anyone you do know?"

"No, Mr. Bransome." Walt wiped an imaginary stain from the counter and looked bored.

"Too bad," said Bransome.

A customer called for attention. Walt moved along the counter, served him, did a bit more perfunctory wiping. Bransome brooded over his cup of coffee. After a while Walt ambled up to his end and offered an afterthought.

"I think that big lug is called Kossy or Kozzy. What is all this, anyway?"

136

"I'm asking to forestall the cops. How did you get his name?"

"I was here one evening and he was squatting by the counter and giving the evil eye to the mirror as usual. Four young fellows came in and sat at that table over there. One of them gave him the hi-ho and called him Kossy or Kozzy. He didn't like it. No, sir, he didn't like it one little bit. He gave this youngster a look of sudden death and dumped his cup and went out. The other fellow laughed and shrugged it off."

"Know who this youngster is?"

"No, I don't. I think I've seen him somewhere before. Probably he's a casual customer who comes in once in a blue moon."

"What about his three pals?"

"Oh, I know one of those—Jim Falkner."

"Stand back and let the dog see the rabbit," said Bransome, putting down his cup and getting off the stool. "Where can I find Jim Falkner?"

"Don't know where he lives, Mr. Bransome, but I can tell you where he works." Another look at the clock. "In Voce's Barber Shop on Bleeker Street. He should be there right now."

"Thanks, Walt. Tonight you will be mentioned in my prayers."

"That's nice," said Walt, giving the ghost of a smile.

Bransome trudged to the barber shop on Bleeker Street, which wasn't far away. It proved to be a small, dingy place with four well-worn chairs and two attendants. Plenty of loose hair lay scattered over the unswept floor. One barber, gray-headed and in his sixties, was trimming a customer in the chair farthest from the door. The other barber was a shrimpish, sallow-faced youth sprawling on a bench by the wall and reading a comic book. As Bransome entered the youth reluctantly got up and motioned toward a chair. Bransome sat in it.

"Short back and sides." When the other had finished he slipped him a tip and whispered, "Want a word with you at the door."

Following him to the entrance, the youth asked in equally low tones, "What's the idea?"

137

"Are you Jim Falkner?"

"Yes—how d'you know my name?"

"Got it from a mutual friend, Walt at the snack bar."

"Oh, that zombie."

"I'm trying to trace a fellow last seen in the diner. He's a big, ugly clunker who's been there only a few times. Walt says you were there one evening with three friends. One of them spoke to this man and got given the conspicuous brush-off. Do you remember that?"

"Sure do. The big bum took off looking sour. Gil laughed and said he was as chummy as a rattlesnake."

"Gil?"

"Gilbert." Suspicion clouded Falkner's face. "What are you after? Are you a cop?"

"Do I look like one? I've lost track of this big character and want to find him. It's a private matter. Gilbert hasn't anything to worry about, I can promise you that. Now, who is he and where can I find him?"

Falkner said a little unwillingly, "His name is Gilbert Mitchell. He's at the Star Garage at the end of this street."

"That's all I want to know. Thanks for the help."

"It's okay," said Falkner, still doubtful about the wisdom of giving away his friends.

Mitchell turned out to be a well-built blond with a fixed half-grin. His hands were black with automobile grease and he had a smear of it across his face. Wiping the face with an even greasier sleeve, he gave Bransome his attention.

"I'm searching for a heavyweight whose name and address I don't know. He was last seen in the station snack bar. Walt says you were there one evening with Jim Falkner and a couple of others. You greeted this character with the name of Kossy or Kozzy and he gave you the cold shoulder. What d'you know about him?"

"Nothing much."

"You did speak to him?"

"I wasted my breath on him."

"Then you must know something about him."

"A fat lot. I've seen him plenty of times in a poolroom downtown. I go there two or three times a week

138

and usually he's there too. Most times he's using the table next to mine. He plays with a tough, deadpan bunch who call him Kossy. That's all I know."

"Where is this poolroom?"

Mitchell obliged with the information.

"About what time does Kossy show up there?"

"It varies. Sometimes he's there early, sometimes late. About nine o'clock would be a good bet." Mitchell's grin widened as he added, "Don't play him for money, mister—you'll get skinned."

"Thanks—I won't."

He had no intention of playing pool with Kossy or with anyone else. His only desire was to get the quarry in sight. What he'd do after that would depend upon circumstances.

The poolroom held twelve tables of which eight were in use. He wandered casually through the smoke-laden atmosphere examining players and spectators, all of whom were too interested in their games to take any notice of him. Nobody was present whom he could recognize.

Arriving at a little shack-like office in one corner, he peered through its doorway. Inside sat a bald-headed man smoking a thin cheroot and playing with the guts of a time-recorder. Several tipless cues were racked against one wall and a box of blue chalks stood open on a tiny desk.

"Happen to know a big pug named Kossy?"

Baldhead looked up, showing lined and liverish features. He extracted the cheroot.

"Why should I tell you?"

Ignoring the question, Bransome opened his wallet, took out a bill. The other made it disappear as if he were performing a conjuring trick. The money vanished but its recipient's expression did not become less vinegary.

"His name is Kostavik," informed Baldhead, speaking without moving his lips. "Lives somewhere nearby. Been coming here only the last five or six weeks but shows up often. Think he moves around quite a lot. Don't know what he does for a living and don't want to. That's about all I can say."

"How about his pals?"

"One of them is called Shas and another Eddy. There's yet another but I've never heard his name used. All of them speak English with an offbeat accent. If they're citizens the ink is still wet on their papers."

"Much obliged." He gave the other a significant look. "Nobody has asked you anything, not a question."

"Nobody ever does." Baldhead rammed the cheroot in his mouth and resumed his fiddling with the time-recorder.

Leaving the poolroom, Bransome crossed the street, settled himself in a doorway and proceeded to keep watch on the place. This was as far as he'd been able to get and he'd have to stay with it. If nobody showed up this evening he'd try again tomorrow and the day after. It was a welcome change to be the chaser instead of the chased.

Already the sky was darkening with impending nightfall and some stores had closed, including the one in the doorway of which he was standing. Lack of sunlight was no handicap; street lamps and neon signs made pedestrians clearly visible on both sides of the street. Desultory traffic was the chief nuisance, because anyone could slip unseen into the poolroom when masked by a passing car or truck. Apart from that he was doing all right provided that no officious cop hustled him onward. He could expect to be given the hard shove sooner or later; cops do not like lurkers in shop doorways.

This thought had hardly crossed his mind when a cop came into view a hundred yards away and on his own side of the road. He watched the blue-clad official figure parading toward him at a slow, deliberate pace and decided that this spying business was not as simple as it seemed. He'd been stationed there a mere ten minutes and now was about to be moved on. So far as he could see there was no way of avoiding it. To leave the doorway at this precise moment would look suspicious. It would be better to remain and wear a dull-witted expression.

Ponderously the cop came on, reached the doorway, lumbered straight past and ostentatiously refrained

140

from seeing him. That was strange indeed. The officer's manner and bearing shouted aloud that he was well aware of Bransome's presence but determined to ignore it. The incident was out of character and contrary to cop-custom. Bransome stared after the retreating figure and was mystified.

Approximately one hour later the cop came back and carefully surveyed all doorways except the one Bransome occupied. At that one he acknowledged the watcher's existence with a grunt and a curt nod. Then he pounded onward, still looking into doorways and occasionally testing locks. Bransome felt like a man who has been awarded a medal without knowing why.

At that point his attention was drawn back to the facing poolroom. Six men were coming out and four going in. He could see the faces of the departees but not those of the arrivals. However, all were of average height and build and obviously did not include the elusive Kostavik.

His vigil ended at eleven-thirty. Three men emerged. With a tremendous thrill of excitement he recognized one as a member of the pair who had caught him in his fall down the steps. The other two were complete strangers. He had not seen this suspect inside the poolroom, neither had he observed him entering it; presumably he must have been among the few who had shown only their backs when going in—and at a time when his own mind was obsessed by thoughts of Kostavik. Temporarily he forgot Kostavik and followed this trio. So far as he was concerned one lead was as good as another.

Chatting together and apparently without a care in the world, the three paced rapidly along the street with Bransome a hundred yards behind and on the opposite side. Farther back two more men came out of an alley and followed Bransome, one on each side of the road. On a corner farther back the cop made a gesture and a car loaded with four men crawed into view and tagged along behind them all.

This weird procession of shadower-plus-shadower wended its way along the road and through several side streets to a major crossing. Here the leading trio stopped, conversed for a minute or two, then split in three directions. Without hesitation Bransome kept grimly after the one he'd recognized.

Behind, the two walking trackers likewise split and went after the pair Bransome had disregarded. The car halted and disgorged one man who hung behind Bransome while it in turn followed at a discreet distance behind him.

Crossing a vacant lot the presumably unsuspecting leader made for a phone booth on a corner, entered it and started dialing. Bransome stopped in the shadow of a high wall and leaned against the brickwork. His follower lolled by a parked car and pretended to be boredly waiting for someone.

The man in the booth got his connection and said, "Kossy, I'm at Slater and Tenth. I'm being tailed. Eh? Feds my eye! This one's so raw he's flashing a red light and ringing a firebell. Whatcha say? Yes, all right—I'll drag him round to Sammy's."

Leaving the booth, he refrained from looking backward. He walked steadily on. Bransome gave him a slightly longer lead and followed. So did the pseudo car-owner.

Soon afterward the shadowing car reached the phone booth and halted. A man got out, called a number, cross-examined somebody. Hurriedly he made a second call and returned to the car.

"This boy is good—if he doesn't get his head blown off before he's through."

"Have any luck?"

"Yes. They pinpointed the other party and I've passed the news along."

The car surged forward, the two leaders of the chase now being out of sight. It didn't matter much: the man on foot was a remaining link and would point the way.

He did, too. After three more streets he stepped from an alley and halted the car. Whispering to those within it, he indicated a graystone apartment house halfway up the road and on the right. Two men got out and joined him. Cautiously the three approached the house. Left to himself, the car's driver felt under the dashboard, drew out a hand-microphone, switched on a radio transmitter and sent out a call. Elsewhere in the

142

city and not far away two more loaded cars started heading fast in his direction.

Without bothering to sneak a look toward Bransome, the man at the head of the multiple pursuit made a sudden turn, ran up four steps and entered the graystone building. His figure became swallowed in the darkness of the interior while the front door remained invitingly open.

Still hugging the opposite side of the road, Bransome maintained his cautious rate of progress, passed the apartment house, stopped on the next corner and considered the situation. To decide his next move was simple enough. Either he must go into that house or stay out of it. If he did the latter the entire chase would become futile unless he kept watch on the place until such time as he could link this character with other suspects he had in mind. He was badly in need of such a linkage because without it he had nothing more than theories and suspicions that in official estimation would smack of the fantastic.

Keeping a given address under expert and constant observation, possibly for several days and nights, was a task more suitable for the police or a detective agency. He had the addresses of two agencies in his pocket right now. But they'd be of little use in these circumstances—like the police, they would not know for whom to look. Descriptions of five men would be their sole data and—after his experiences with the two trucking companies—he had little faith in verbal pictures. The blunt fact remained that only he, Bransome, could recognize certain characters on sight. Therefore he must handle the job himself as best he could.

To hang around all through the night would try his patience, which was elastic enough for dealing with scientific problems but lacked stretching qualities in the matter of sweet retribution. Besides, this evening he had found definite suggestion of a link: he had staked out the poolroom in hope of tracing one man and had found another. At least two of them, therefore, must be frequenting the same playground.

Inside this nearby pile of masonry might be a third

143

member of the bunch. Or even all five or six of them, gabbing and plotting together and laughing over their beer. Yes, grinning like apes because other and better men had become burdened with imaginary corpses.

As anger mounted within him he knew he just had to go in there and take a chance. For the first time in his life he wished he had a gun. Yet a weapon need not be essential. If prowlers who were none too bright could enter bedrooms and rifle the pockets of sleepers, surely he could sneak around long enough to learn a few things and escape unharmed.

He would go inside, creep quietly from floor to floor and try to discover the identities of the various apartment owners who, in all probability, would have their names upon their doors. If one of them proved to be an elephant named Kostavik it would be linkage enough to justify running out and phoning the police and inviting them to come and stop the riot. Then he'd return to start the said affray.

Going back to the graystone building, he mounted its steps, went through the door, found himself in a long, narrow hall dimly lit at the back by one feeble bulb. The hall ended in a narrow staircase with a small elevator at its side. Four apartment doors opened onto the hall. This floor was silent, as if unoccupied, but he could hear faint noises of movement above. From higher still came the muffled sound of a radio playing the *Radetsky March*. The whole place was scruffy, with peeling paint on the walls, woodwork chipped and scratched, a musty smell in the air.

As quietly as possible he moved from door to door and read the names thereon. In the poor light he almost had to put his nose to them. He was peering closely at a grubby card pinned to the door nearest the rear of the hall, and had time only to note that it said Samuel someone-or-other, when the door whisked open and a violent thrust in the small of the back boosted him through it headlong.

The double event took him so completely by surprise that he went into the room at an off-balance run, and heard the door slam behind him just as he toppled and buried his face in the threadbare carpet. A series of ultra-rapid thoughts flashed through his mind even as

144

he fell. A shove like that must be deliberate and with malice aforethought. Whoever had slipped up behind him was a tough customer who meant business. This was no time for professions of mistakes, explanations and apologies. Whatever could be done had better be done good and fast.

So he thumped the carpet, rolled like mad, glimpsed a pair of columnar legs, wrapped his arms around the ankles, heaved with all his might and gained himself a playmate on the floor. The room shook as the other's bulk hit the floorboards. It was Kossy.

Somebody with evil intent was bending over Bransome but found himself thwarted by Kossy's downfall and the resulting struggle. He spat a guttural oath, danced around seeking a vantage point, caught one of the violently thrashing Kossy's big boots on his knee-cap. He swore again and dropped something that rang like a tire iron.

Kossy had good reason for waving his heavy limbs around. His big, florid face reached the carpet, at which point Bransome recognized it. Unable to make a hefty swing while in a prone position, Bransome did the next best thing. He clutched Kossy's neck in a grip good enough to stay fixed until death us do part and dug his thumbs into the other's windpipe.

A few weeks ago he'd never have believed himself capable of taking sadistic pleasure in trying to strangle someone. But that was what he was doing right now, forcing his thumbs with furious violence partly derived from justifiable resentment and partly from the knowledge that his opponent was plenty big enough to eat him if given half a chance. An alliance of fear and anger was lending him power such as he had never possessed.

So he strove mightily to force his thumbs through Kossy's gullet and out the back of his neck while all the time his brain but not his voice kept reiterating, "I'll give you Arline, you big, fat bastard! I'll give you Arline!"

Kossy's hairy, spadelike hands clamped on Bransome's wrists and tried to tear away his grip, but he held on so determinedly that the other merely pulled his own head forward. They threshed violently around

145

with Kossy slowly purpling. The third man ceased cursing, grabbed Bransome's hair and tried to tear his scalp from his cranium. The recent haircut deprived the assailant of enough grip and his fingers slid free. He then clutched Bransome's shoulders to try to tear him loose from the supine Kossy. Bransome kicked like a mule, made connection somewhere and heard a yelp of agony as the pulling hands let go.

The shouts and sounds of struggling caused another door in the hall to open. There was an incoming rush of feet but Bransome could not look up because his full attention was on his opponent. By now Kossy's chest was heaving with wheezy, bronchial noises and he was striving to jerk a huge knee into Bransome's groin.

Then a number of rough hands simultaneously seized Bransome and tore him away by main force. He was pulled erect. A hard and horny hand slapped his face several times, swiftly and brutally, with force that dazed him and made him reel backward.

Dimly he was aware of sounds all around, heavy breathing and muttered curses, the shift of many feet. A heavy blow on one ear made his mind whirl. He blinked his eyes in effort to focus and couldn't see Kossy anywhere, but in a hazy sort of way did see a group of faces one of which was that of a pseudo-trucker, the fellow who'd had so much to say about bones near Burleston. He lashed out to hit that face with everything he could muster, and felt the hard crack of knuckles landing on the other's mouth.

Then a mess of stars exploded in his left eye and he went down for the second time. He fell knowing that he had made a major blunder in entering this building and would be denied the chance ever to make another mistake. There were at least six men in the room, all ruthless. The odds were far too heavy. He'd had his fun and this was the payoff. One does strange things in desperate moments; his was to emit a sigh of regret as he hit the floor.

Somebody either jumped on him or kicked the breath out of him. Wind expelled from his lungs and stomach in one great whoosh. Instinctively he knew that the next vicious wallop would break a rib but he was too near the knockout to roll sideways and avoid it. Per-

146

force he waited for it, lying flat on his back and fighting for air.

There sounded a loud thumping in the hall, followed by the crash of a door, a waft of cool night air and a harsh voice that bawled, "Hold it!"

Resulting silence almost could be felt. The rib-shattering kick did not arrive. Making a gigantic effort, Bransome turned over, face downward, and tried to be sick. Failing, he turned back, struggled into a half-sitting position, nursed his stomach and stared blearily out of one eye. He had been wrong; his opponents numbered not six but eight. They stood together in a glowering bunch, facing him but looking at the doorway behind his back. They posed like figures in a waxworks, stiff, unspeaking, motionless.

Hands slid under Bransome's armpits. He came slowly to his feet with the hands helping him upward. For a moment his legs felt rubbery and about to give way but strength flowed back into them. He turned around and saw four men in plain clothes and one uniformed cop, all holding guns. One of the former was Reardon.

Unable to think of anything suitable to the occasion, Bransome said, "Hi!" Then it struck him that nothing could have sounded more silly. He smirked with the uninjured side of his face, the other side refusing to co-operate.

Reardon refused to see the humor of it. He spoke sourly. "You all right?"

"No—I feel like death warmed up."

"Want hospital attention?"

"I'm not that bad. Only knocked around a bit. Give me time and I'll be okay."

"You sure asked for what you got," Reardon opined. "First you refuse us a chance of getting anywhere. Next you want it all to yourself. Look what it's bought you."

"Would have bought me a damn sight more if you hadn't rushed in."

"Lucky for you that we did." Reardon turned to the man in uniform, made a gesture at the silent eight. "That's the wagon by the sound of it. Take 'em away."

147

By now blank-faced and impassive, the eight departed. Not even Kossy showed the slightest expression as he went out. He was massaging his throat and holding his mouth open like a hungry carp, but for all the emotion he displayed he might have been caught in the act of reciting his prayers.

Reardon's sharp eyes examined the room before he spoke to the men in plain clothes. "Right, boys, give this dump the treatment. Go through every other apartment as well. If any amateur lawyer yaps about search warrants, book him on suspicion and bring him in. Make a thorough job of it and pull down the walls if you have to. Phone me at headquarters if and when you find anything that looks good." Then he signed to Bransome. "You come with me, Sherlock."

Bransome obediently followed, full of aches and pains and a little dizzy. Clambering into the rear seat of the car, he grunted with agony as he bumped a bruise, and gently rubbed the side of his face. His cheekbone burned and throbbed, and he had a fat eye, a thick ear and a split lip. His stomach felt full of little green apples and his whole abdomen was sore. If Dorothy could see me now, he thought, there'd be hell to pay.

Getting into the front seat, Reardon had a few words with the driver, and used the radio before they moved off. Three more prowl-cars were now lined up outside the graystone building and a small crowd of curious spectators had gathered around, some in their night-clothes. The car sped along the street. Cocking an elbow over the back of his seat, Reardon twisted to one side to address his passenger.

"If I wanted to know the characteristics of alloy-creep at very high temperature, I'd come and ask you. If you want to know who's looking through your bedroom keyhole, you're supposed to come and ask me."

Bransome said nothing.

"As a scientist I don't doubt that you're highly competent," Reardon went on. "But as a crook you're a dumb bum. And as a detective you stink."

"Thanks!" said Bransome, glumly.

"When you dived out of that train you might have killed yourself. A stupid thing to do. And it served no

148

useful purpose that I can see. Certainly it did not get us off your neck."

"No?"

"No! From that moment we had you located within a theoretical progress-circle that expanded hour by hour. We knew that some segments were likelier than others because of better transport facilities." He paused, hung on as the car swung around a sharp corner. "Chief Pascoe had been asked to report without delay any odd datum remotely concerning Burleston. So when he called us long-distance and said that someone had been asking about an unknown murder there and we found that the query came from a point on the main route back here—"

"You put two and two together, eh?"

"And made it four. It was highly unlikely that anyone else but you would call from that particular place at that particular time to chew the fat about mysterious bones said to have been dug up near Burleston. Didn't need second sight to tell us who Robert Lafarge was—he was the same chump as Lucius Carter. We began to see daylight. In effect, you were telling us by proxy what you had refused to confess face to face, namely, that you had—or believed you had—a killing on your conscience."

Bransome grimly nursed his bruises and offered no comment.

"It made everything add up," Reardon continued. "Yet there was no such crime. Pascoe vouched for that. What's more, he'd told you as much. It made your resultant moves obvious. Having got rid of a deadly burden on your mind, you'd be wildly delighted or coldly furious, according to the state of your liver. In either case you'd head back here. If delighted, you'd return to the bosom of your family and forget everything. If on the boil you'd come back to try to take it out of somebody's pants. We couldn't do anything about it ourselves because we didn't know the identity of that somebody. But *you* did—and *you* could lead us to him. We watched incoming trains, buses and cars. It was easy to pick you up at the station and wander around with you."

"I didn't see anyone following me." Bransome

149

tenderly licked a lip that seemed as thick as a rubber tire and rapidly growing thicker.

"You weren't supposed to see. We don't make a sloppy job of it." Reardon bared his teeth at him. "You didn't go home. You ran around thirsting for blood. That suited us topnotch. You got a lead from that coffee-slinger in the snack bar, then from the skinny runt in the barber shop, then from the oily boy at the garage. When finally you took root outside that poolroom we figured that you were all set to point to somebody for us—and you did!"

"Two of them skipped," said Bransome, seeking some small source of satisfaction. "I couldn't follow three ways at once."

"We could and we did. They'll be grabbed after they've taken us wherever they're going."

The cruiser pulled in alongside an office building with lights showing only on the second floor. Reardon got out, Bransome following. Entering the building, they disregarded the elevators and used the stairs, passed many clearly lit offices, and reached one marked only by a number on its door. The entire floor had the air of being active twenty-four hours per day, seven days a week.

Taking a chair, Bransome gazed around, seeing with one eye and half-seeing with the other. "This doesn't look like police headquarters."

"Because it isn't. The police are called in as and when required. Espionage, sabotage and other crimes against the constitution are our business, not theirs." Seating himself behind a desk, Reardon flipped an intercom switch. "Send in Casasola."

A man arrived within a minute. He was young, olive-skinned and had the brisk air of a doctor with little time to waste.

Reardon nodded toward the battered-looking Bransome. "This man has been deservedly mauled. Patch him up and make him resemble a human being."

Casasola smiled and led Bransome along a corridor to a first-aid room. There he set to work and painted the rainbow around Bransome's eye, sealed the split lip, and swabbed the thick ear and swollen cheek with an ice-cold liquid. He worked swiftly and in silence, obviously accustomed to repairing the beaten-up at any hour of the day or night. By the time he'd finished and returned the patient to the office, Reardon was fidgeting in his chair.

"You still look like something the cat dragged in," he greeted. He waved toward a wall clock. "It's the unearthly hour of two o'clock and still we're on the job. By the looks of it we're going to be horsing around all night."

"Why? Has something else happened?"

"Yes. Those other two fugitives led us to a couple more addresses. There's been some strife at one of them. A copper's been hurt. Got a slug through his paw. They took four prisoners. I'm still waiting to hear about the other address. Maybe it'll blow up when they knock."

He scowled at the desk-phone, which must have felt sensitive about it because it promptly shrilled. Reardon snatched it up.

"Who? McCracken? Yes? Three more, eh? What's that? A mess of apparatus? Don't bother to try to make head or tail of it. I'm coming out right away with experts competent to handle it. Send in those three and keep a guard on the joint." He reached for a scrap of paper. "Give me that address again." Racking the phone, he stuffed the paper into his pocket and stood up. "I think this is the end of the trail. You'd better come along."

"Suits me," said Bransome. "Might find somebody else I can sock in the jaw."

"You'll do nothing of the kind," Reardon asserted. "I'm taking you in the hope that you can tell us something about this apparatus. We want to know exactly what it is, how it works and what it does."

"I'll be a big help. I know nothing about it."

"You must know something. Maybe when you see it you'll wake up and remember."

Calling at another office on their way out, they picked up two men named Saunders and Waite. The former was middle-aged, plump and ponderous; the

151

latter elderly, thoughtful and myopic. Both had the quiet self-assurance of characters who'd never had trouble estimating the number of beans in a bottle.

They piled into a cruiser, which took them at a fast pace across town to a tiny warehouse and office located in an obscure back street. A big-jowled, over-muscled individual opened the door and looked out as they pulled up.

"Mac's taken away the three we found here," he informed Reardon as they went inside. He jerked a thumb toward the door at the back of the office. "Two were asleep in there, snoring like hogs. The other was the mug who led us here. They took a dim view of being snatched. We had to ruin their health somewhat."

"Anyone else shown up since?"

"Not a soul."

"Somebody might before morning. Have to get two or three more men. We'll need a better welcome committee." Reardon gazed around expectantly. "Where's this gadgetry Mac was talking about?"

"Through there." Again he indicated the rear door.

Reardon shoved it open and went through, the others following. Dirty and tattered posters on the walls showed that once upon a time the warehouse had held toys and cheap fancy goods. Now it was divided by plasterboard partitions to provide a sleeping room for three, a small and roughly furnished recreation room with kitchen and toilet attached and, finally, a section holding the apparatus.

Standing in a row, they examined the shiny contraption. Its insides were concealed behind detachable casings that would have to be unbolted to reveal its mechanism. It stood six feet high by six long by three wide and may have weighed a couple of tons. A pair of hooded lenses projected from its front and an electric motor was linked to its back. The lenses were aimed at a black velvet curtain hung on the facing wall.

Reardon said to Saunders and Waite, "Get busy on it and see what you can discover. You can have as long as you need—but the sooner we know, the better. If you want me I'll be in the office."

Motioning to Bransome, he led him back to where the

152

guard was sitting in semi-darkness with his attention on the front door.

The guard said, "We won't get any more rats scuttling into this hole. The prowl-car outside is a give-away."

"I know." Reardon dumped himself behind a dilapidated desk and put his feet up on it. "Take it away and bring back two or three more men. Dump the car out of sight a few streets along and leave a man in charge—we don't want it pinched while we're resting our corns here. Get the others as soon as you can. I guess there'll be enough of us then."

"Right!" The guard opened the door and departed. They heard the car roar away.

Bransom asked, "Enough of us for what?"

"Until we've finished questioning the characters we've grabbed, we won't know whether their mob numbers twenty or two hundred. It's possible that we've got all of them but we can't be sure about it. Any still running loose are likely to take alarm when they call the roll and find a number missing. In that event they may rush here to remove or destroy that contraption in the back. Or they may abandon it and take to the boats and planes. I don't know what the heck they'll do —but I can't overlook a possible attempt to swipe the evidence."

"I suppose you're right."

Reardon bent toward him, eyes intent. "Do you remember this dump?"

"No."

"Well, did you recognize that apparatus?"

"No, I didn't."

"You absolutely sure you've never seen it before?"

"Not that I can recall." The other's disappointment was so visible that Bransome raked his mind in effort to dig up a vague memory. "I've a queer feeling that it ought to be familiar to me—but it isn't."

"Humph!"

They went silent. The office remained without lights lest illumination scare off wanted visitors, but a street lamp shining through the upper windows gave gloomy visibility within. For three hours they waited, during which time two more guards arrived and sat with them. At five o'clock in the morning someone rattled the front door and tried its lock. A guard whipped it open, gun in hand, while the others shot to their feet. It was only the cop on the beat.

Twenty minutes later Waite appeared from the back. He was holding in his right hand a long, dangling strip of shiny substance. His features were strained and his glasses sat halfway down his nose.

"That thing in there," he announced, "should not be used on a dog. It's a stroboscopic horror. The fellow who thought it up would do the world a favor by having his head amputated."

Reardon demanded, "What does it do?"

"Half a minute." Waite eyed the back door.

Saunders came through, sat on the edge of the desk, and mopped his plump face with a handkerchief. His complexion was dark red and he looked far from happy.

"Being forewarned and not drugged, I got away with it. Otherwise I certainly wouldn't." Saunders wiped his face again. "In that torture-chamber I've just killed a fellow. I finished him off good and proper and I did it with the greatest gusto. I pinned him on his bed and cut his throat from ear to ear."

"That's right," chipped in Waite. "It was a deliberate and thoroughly cold-blooded murder, as juicy a crime as you could witness in a thousand years. There was one thing wrong with it."

"Namely?" asked Reardon studying him beady-eyed.

"He couldn't possibly have committed it—because I did it myself. Ear to ear, just like that!"

Unimpressed by these rival claims to bloody slaughter, Reardon said, "Same victim, same place, same technique, same motive?"

"Of course. Same picture." Waite waved the shiny strip around. "This is a slice of the killing. Take a look at it." He tossed it onto the desk. "That gadget in the back room is a very special movie projector. It throws a stereoscopic picture in natural colors. The image is shown on a screen composed of thousands of

154

tiny pyramid-shaped beads and the three-dimensional effect is visible without need of polarized glasses."

"Nothing new in that," scoffed Reardon. "It's been done before."

"There's more to it," explained Waite. "First, the picture is made so that the camera identifies itself with the audience. Its viewpoint is that of the onlooker."

"That's been done too."

"Second, it runs frames in side-by-side pairs with three-inch angular shift to give the stereoscopic effect. The frames aren't standard 35-mm stuff. They're a bastard caliber. They whiz through at three thousand three hundred frames a minute. At every fifth frame the illumination momentarily boosts sky-high. The result is intense light-flare at the rate of eleven pulses per second—which approximates the natural rhythm of the optic nerves. Know what that means?"

"No—go on."

"It's the rotating mirror effect all over again. The pulsations shove the viewer into a state of hypnosis."

"Hell!" said Reardon. He held up the strip of film and examined it by the light of the outside street-lamp.

Waite offered, "Unless he's been doped—and it's highly likely that a victim of this gadget would first be doped—the viewer starts seeing the picture knowing full well that it is only a picture. But he soon slides into a condition of hypnosis after which, in effect, he becomes the camera. Or, if you like it better, the camera becomes himself. His mind is then compelled to accept and register a false memory. The brain just won't accommodate it in a time and place where a contrary memory already exists. However, plenty of empty spaces are available, those being attributable to times in the past when one experienced nothing worth remembering. This apparatus creates the crime, the characters, the motive, the place, the circumstances and the approximate period in the past. It gets rammed into the brain and fills a previously empty place where, for one reason or another, nothing has been recorded."

"It would seem incredible to anyone who hadn't experienced the results," put in Bransome, a trifle morbidly, "but I know to my cost how really convincing the effect can be."

"What it all boils down to," said Waite, "is that some unknown genius has devised fully automated brainwashing. It's plenty good enough to convince anyone that black is white—provided, of course, that he's been caught off-guard and doesn't know what is being done to him." Feeling in his pocket, he brought out another short length of film and gave it to Bransome. "There's a small movie-library in that torture-chamber. It has a file of ready-made killings. They're located all over the place, anywhere from here to Timbuctu. One of them is tagged Burleston though in all likelihood it wasn't made within a thousand miles of there. How d'you like it?"

Bransome held it up to the poor light. "Holy smoke, that's Arline!"

"Probably a small-time actress on the other side of the planet," suggested Reardon.

"I doubt it," countered Saunders, speaking for the first time in a while. He was still perspiring. "Those murders are far too real. I've a sickening feeling that the leading characters literally acted themselves to death."

"That's what I think," agreed Waite.

"How d'you mean?" Reardon pressed.

"The deaths are far too plausible to be faked. My guess is that certain people were marked down for permanent removal. But instead of being subjected to summary execution they were kidded along and taken for suckers. Each was persuaded to play his or her part in a movie and discovered too late that the last scene was in deadly earnest."

Reardon thought it over. "I wouldn't put it beyond some people."

"Neither would I," said Waite. "Death itself can be made useful to the state. Anyway, the technique is a heller because those who become loaded with guilt are thereby given every inducement not to talk. What can you do to help a man who finds himself a hidey-hole and determinedly conceals the fact that something has gone wrong inside his skull?"

"I know, I know." Reardon threw a meaningful look at Bransome. He consulted his watch. "We'll have that

156

gadget taken away for further examination. No use us hanging around here any longer." Then to Bransome, "You'll come with us to headquarters. We'll give you eight hours' sleep and any meals you want. Then you'll tell us your story in complete detail and identify those you can of the characters we've caught. After that you can go home."

At six o'clock in the evening Reardon drove him home, conversing on the way. "There's no doubt you were picked on as the easiest mark in the particular circumstances of that day. You were slugged, drugged and transported to the operating theater. They gave you the treatment. Then they carted you back to the steps, shook you awake, patted your face and sympathized with you. A few days later another guy triggered the effect and got you on the run."

"That's how it was," admitted Bransome. "It's a pity I didn't get more curious about those two missing hours."

"You were confused. The sludge that you think with had been stirred up and mauled around and you were muddle-minded." Reardon mused a bit, went on, "Now there's all the other victims to be rounded up. They don't know they've been haunted and that the ghosts have been laid. How're we going to cope with them? How're we going to make sure that all this doesn't happen again? The gang we've collared may be only the first of several mobs making ready to function elsewhere."

"The solution's easy," Bransome declared. "Hold me up as a horrid example. Tell everyone what has happened to me and how and why. I don't mind—I'd be a good antidote. The scientific mind appreciates a clever trick even when it's a dirty one. Scientists are more concerned with ingenuity than with ethics."

"Think that'll bring back the others?"

"Sure thing. They'll return looking thoroughly sheepish. And they'll be so annoyed they'll spend hours trying to concoct a bigger and better counterstroke. Sooner or later they'll invent one. Thirst for revenge is a pretty good driving force." He glanced at his listener and invited, "There's one thing you have not told me, one thing I'd like to know—exactly *who* was behind all these shenanigans?"

"Sorry, I mustn't say. There's a complete clampdown on basic information. I can give you two items for your own satisfaction. First, three officials of a certain embassy are leaving by plane tonight at our urgent request. Second, nobody is going to give you a medal—but you're likely to find your pay check a bit larger."

"Well, that's something. I think I've earned it."

"I don't. I think there's no justice in this world." The car slid to a stop outside Bransome's house. Reardon got out with him and accompanied him to the door. When Dorothy appeared Reardon said rapidly, "I've brought back the runaway battered but still whole. I've promised him a pay-raise and that entitles me to a large whiskey. I'd appreciate it now."

Taken aback, Dorothy hurried to get it.

Holding the glass high, Reardon looked pointedly at both of them, said, "Here's to murder!" and downed the drink.

The phone shrilled, Dorothy answered it, called to Bransome, "Somebody for you." She edged away, watching Reardon warily. Bransome grinned at her and picked up the phone.

A voice bawled excitedly, "Bransome, you were dead right. I'm in the clear. Did you hear what I said? I'm in the clear! We've got to look into this together, Bransome. We can't let things rest as they are. I'm on my way back and will arrive at ten-thirty. Can you meet me?"

"Don't worry—I'll be there." He cradled the phone and said to Reardon, "That was Henderson. He's due back at ten-thirty and is all set to do some scalping."

"We'll pick him up the moment he shows his face. He can do some identifying for us." He eyed the whiskey bottle. "I think that's worth celebrating too. What're we waiting for?"

Dorothy, still mystified, filled his glass and he raised it saying, "Here's to another murder!"

Bransome's gaze included both Reardon and the drink. "Not for me, thanks!" he said wearily.

158